CAPTAIN WIRGOIL'S
CHALLENGE

A short adult fiction written by:

ALAN F DAVIES

MAPLE
PUBLISHERS

Captain Wirgoil's Challenge

Author: Alan F Davies

First Published in 2021

ISBN 978-1-914366-28-4 (Paperback)
     978-1-914366-29-1 (Ebook)

Book cover design and Book layout by:
    White Magic Studios
    www.whitemagicstudios.co.uk

Published by:
    Maple Publishers
    1 Brunel Way,
    Slough,
    SL1 1FQ, UK
    www.maplepublishers.com

A CIP catalogue record for this title is available from the British Library.

The Dedication

This story is dedicated to our beautiful granddaughters Serena and Vicky who sadly lost their challenge in life.

THE CHAPTERS

Chapter One: THE TRAMP

A tramp is walking along a remote hillside road somewhere in Cornwall, England. The tramp is pushing an old babies' pram that he found dumped somewhere many months ago while he was walking the roads of England. In the pram he keeps his meagre possessions that enable him to stay alive.

As he walks along the dusty road the right front wheel of the pram is wobbling and has a distinctive squeak, which is the only sound that can be heard apart from his heavy breathing and occasional cough. The tramp who prefers to be nameless is suffering from the effects of living a life out in the open in all weathers. His mind has become fragmented into sometimes being in a reality world, and sometimes being in a fantasy world. At this moment in time the tramp is in his fantasy world. He believes that his pram is a real person, and he's named it Albert.

The tramp is walking along the road, very slowly. He's hunched up over Albert's rusty handle. He's constantly talking to Albert, telling him of all his troubles - he pretends or maybe really believes that Albert is talking back to him.

The tramp is not in any hurry, because he's not going anywhere in particular. He's on this road today for no reason. It's just another road, just like the last road, and the one before that.

As he walks he's muttering the same words over and over again.

"I want to be rich, Albert- I want to be rich, Albert." But it's hard to imagine how this person's wish could ever come true.

It's difficult to tell how old this man is, because he has long unkempt hair and beard that covers most of his face. His hair and beard are showing plenty of grey but it could still be seen that his hair was once blond. His clothes are ragged and dirty and have the appearance like they never really ever belonged to him - his shoes are worn out and one size too big for him; he's padded them out with paper to make them fit his feet.

His body odour indicates that he hasn't washed for quite some time. His sad bloodshot blue eyes tell their own story. This man is showing signs of sleep deprivation. Every now and again he staggers for a few steps. It's like his brain has missed his thoughts. It's clear that this person is nearing the end of his short life.

Some people would feel sorry for this man, but in the cold light of day nobody should, because this man is quite evil. He brought this way of life upon himself - he now rants that he wants to be rich but that's what got him into this situation.

He's been on the run from the police for over two years. This wandering nomad tried to rob a bank - he tried to be rich but he didn't want to work for his money. His plans all went wrong. He didn't get rich, and he hurt some people who were only trying to protect themselves from him.

If he's ever caught he won't see the outside world for a considerable time. But that's not in his mind at the moment; it's all been forgotten. He's wiped it clean from his thoughts. All that matters to him now is surviving in a world that doesn't much care for him.

*

It's the last day of May 1969.10:30am. It's a beautiful warm sunny morning. The tramp can see the sea from his hillside road - suddenly his eyes are drawn to a dirt track that seemed to appear from nowhere, but his eyes are tired, and he's not sure whether it's really there or not.

He rubs his eyes and finds out that it really is there. He has no intention of going down the path, it's very narrow, it's just big enough for him and Albert to go down.

He tries to walk past but Albert is pulling him towards the path - it's clear that Albert wants to go down it. Maybe this was always Albert's role in this sad man's life?

Maybe the tramp was meant to find the pram - the pram was the guider to the pathway.

The tramp is trying his hardest to not go down it but his hands are stuck to Albert's handle, and Albert won't let him go. The tramp shouts, "Albert let me go, I don't want to go down the path." But Albert isn't listening. He's pulling harder, and harder. The tramp has no choice but to follow.

He now finds himself on the path with Albert but he soon realises that this is no ordinary path - it's becoming steeper and steeper. His hands are no longer stuck to the pram handle. He's finding it hard to hold onto Albert on this steep path.

The tramp would like to go back but he can't, because there is no back!! The path is disappearing behind him as he walks - it's like he's being lured towards something. He can see a thick dark mist in the distance that has come off the sea - it seemed to spring up very quickly. The sea mist is rapidly coming towards him. All the time it's getting colder and colder as it approaches. It quickly engulfs him - it's freezing mist, which is surprising, it being a very hot and sunny morning. The tramp has no choice but to stand still. He's shivering and doesn't know what to do. He's wondering what is going on.

It's pitch dark now. He can't go anywhere until this mist clears. Cold moisture is running all down his shivering body. His nose and hair are dripping with the cold water mist that has engulfed him. In a matter of seconds the mist passes and disperses, and it's warm again now.

The tramp is glad that it's gone.

He carries on down the path but with each step that he takes he finds the path getting increasingly steeper. He soon finds himself jogging with Albert. But then he has to run. The pram is becoming too heavy for the tramp to hold onto. He has no choice and has to let go of Albert. He shouts out, "I'm sorry! I'm sorry!"

Albert quickly rolls away, and is soon out of sight. All the tramp can hear is the sound from the squeaky wheel. Which soon fades away in the distance.

The tramp is now running flat out, and is gasping for breath. He won't be able to carry on much longer. A minute or so later he comes to the end of the path where there is a rusty old iron gate.

The tramp cannot stop himself. He crashes into the gate and falls to the ground in considerable pain.

After several minutes he finally sits up, moaning to himself about what has just happened to him.

He's still gasping for breath and is rubbing the sore parts of his body that came in contact with the gate. He slowly gets to his feet. He's lost his old shoes that came off somewhere when he was running down the pathway.

The tramp looks at the gate. It marks the entrance through solid rock that leads into somewhere.

The gate is closed. Its hinges are so corroded that it would seem unlikely that this gate could ever open again. It's not possible for him to climb over it, and there's no way around it. The pathway has gone, it's sheer cliffs behind him. He has to go forward but he cannot see how.

In desperation he pushes the gate and shouts out, "Let me in." He's not expecting anything to happen but to his surprise the gate slowly starts to open all by itself. There's a horrible grating noise of metal against metal as the gate slowly swings open.

The tramp stands there in a state of shock, and doesn't know what is happening. He knows he has to go through the gate but is worried at what he might find on the other side. He wonders where Albert is, because there's no sign of him here, and this was the only way in.

He walked through the gate. As soon as he's through, the gate slammed shut with a loud thud, and then disappeared.

The tramp finds himself in a fairly large cove but wonders why he didn't see it from the top of the hillside road. Even more surprising, there's a village here. None of this did he see from the road. He rubs his weary eyes again, but it doesn't go away - it really is here. To his left, he can see a very old church. Its roof is misshapen, the tiles are out of line - it has the look as if at any minute the roof could fall inside the building.

The tramp is intrigued by what is happening. He walks over to the church to get a better look at it- it's no more than twenty yards away. The church has three small arched windows with old biblical stained glass scenes. There's a rectangular frontage at the entrance to the church. At the top there's a steeple. Two big arched oak doors are the entrance to this dilapidated building.

The tramp went to the doors but they're locked. So he decided to walk around the back to see if there's another way into the church. It led him to a grave yard. He could see that some of the grave stones were very old, but some looked fairly recent. Inscriptions were on the stones. He read one of them. It said:

Here lies Captain Wirgoil
Died of the challenge 1726

The tramp scratched his head not because it was itching but in thought. "I wonder who Captain Wirgoil was? I've never heard of any disease called *challenge.* Ah, here's another stone, I'll see what that says."

Here lies Captain Wirgoil
Died of the challenge 1834

"That's strange, he's got the same name as the other man, and he died of the same thing but it's a different date - how can that be? This is very odd. I don't know what the challenge is but I wouldn't like to catch it."

The tramp walked to another stone. It looked to be newer than the other two stones. He read it and staggered backwards in shock.

Here lies Captain Wirgoil
Died of the challenge 1946

"1946? That's only twenty-three years ago. I wonder what this challenge is?"

The tramp scampered around the gravestones looking at every stone, every single one of them was a Captain Wirgoil, and they had all died of the challenge.

"So there are people here, but where are they? And why are they all called Captain Wirgoil?" muttered the tramp as he looked at other grave stones. He then came across a stone that looked very recent - 1968 read the inscription. This stone worried the tramp.

He walked back to the front of the church - his brain was alert now, he was intrigued as to what was happening, none of it made any sense. A pathway that appeared from nowhere, and then disappeared as he went down it - a huge rusty iron gate that couldn't possibly be opened ever again, opened by itself - a cove with a village, appeared from nowhere, and everybody that is buried here is called Captain Wirgoil, and they all died of a mysterious thing called the challenge.

At the front of the church above its entrance was a clock, but it looked like it hadn't worked in years. It still had its hands though. The old clock read that it was 1.13 but he didn't know if it had stopped on am or pm. The tramp had in his pocket an old base metal pocket watch that he had found in a dustbin -

it worked alright despite being a bit battered. He looked at the watch. It read that it was 11:15am so the old church clock was definitely not working. Just to make sure, he stood there for several minutes looking at the clock's hands and they didn't move.

The tramp stood and stared at all the things around him. Everything looked and felt horrible to him. He wished that Albert was here with him. He had already noticed as soon as he had walked through the old gate that there was something very disturbing about this place. There were lots, and lots of human bones, skulls everywhere, and no matter which way he turned the skulls were always facing him - it was like they were watching him! And the sand was blood stained. Old weapons were lying on the ground, some still attached to the hands of the once people who held them in the last fateful moments of their lives. The tramp was not an expert on weaponry but he'd seen similar weapons to what he was looking at, in pirate films - so he knew that these weapons were hundreds of years old.

It was obvious that a battle had been fought here, and it appeared by what he could see that it had been fought out by pirates. The tramp couldn't understand what this place was - it appeared to be an old coastal village, maybe three to four hundred years old but it had been left in the past, which he found very odd. Why hadn't anybody cleaned this place up? - was deep in his thoughts.

He could see plenty of cottage-like buildings a short distance away and decided to investigate.

He walked along a path towards the cottages, and as he walked he could see what appeared to be a sign on his right, just thirty yards up the path. He walked to the sign; it was so dusty that he could not read what it said. He put his hand into his pocket and took out a rather dirty piece of rag that he used as a handkerchief and wiped the sign. Slowly it started to reveal a name. He was hoping that it would reveal the name of this village, but once again it was something very disturbing. The sign read:

THE VILLAGE OF THE LOST SOULS

The tramp had a dilapidated map book in his pocket, and tried to find this village, but no such place was recorded. According to his map book this place didn't exist. The tramp carried on walking toward the buildings that he could see. He came across four shops which were all joined together, and they appeared to show signs of life. This excited the tramp; he now knew that there must be people here. The shops looked to be well stocked.

The first one was a butcher's. Fresh meat was hanging on hooks in the front of the shop window. The tramp could see rabbits, geese, and pigeons, not really what the people of today eat but he didn't mind that; to him, it was food. He could smell fresh baked bread from the second shop. He peered through its window and could see cakes and delicious looking bread set out. The third shop was a green grocer's. There were apples, greengages, plums and other fruits displayed.

The fourth shop wasn't a shop but an inn. The tramp could smell fresh beer being brewed.

He was very hungry and thirsty now. The smell and sight of all this produce had activated his senses, and despite it being late in the morning, all the shops and inn were closed, and there wasn't any indication as to what time they opened.

The tramp was desperate. He hadn't eaten for days, and was starving. He couldn't wait any longer. He banged on the door of the first shop - the butcher's, but there was no answer. He went to the second and third shops but once again nobody responded to his bangs on the doors.

He went to the inn, his mouth dribbling with the thought of a glass of beer but there was nobody there either.

This annoyed the tramp. He decided to take a walk around to see if he could find somebody.

He walked to what appeared to be the main part of the village. He could see rows of ancient cottages. It was so quiet that you could hear a pin drop. There was no sign of any life here at all.

He still hadn't seen any people, and there was nothing growing here. There were no trees - no grass - no flowers - there weren't even any weeds. He hadn't seen any animals, any birds- not even a fly!!

The village appeared to be completely dead. This puzzled him, because there were the three shops and the inn, which indicated there must be somebody living here, but where were the people? He started to look inside the old cottages. Every one that he went into showed the signs of a battle, everything was smashed and skeletons were inside some of the cottages.

He didn't much like it here so he wandered out of the village.

He happened to look up towards the top of the cliff. Half way up, his eyes caught sight of what appeared to be a high wall. The tramp thought that there might be a castle behind it. He approached the cliff face to see if there was a way up to the wall. He wandered along the cliff bottom for several minutes, and came upon some steps that led up to the wall. This excited him, He started to ascend the steps. The steps were narrow and steep, and lying everywhere were bones. He walked slowly up, and up the steps, every step he took was leaving him out of breath. He was soon gasping for air, but finally he reached the top.

At the top there was a gap. The gap had once been filled by gates that could now be seen lying on the ground. They appeared to have been knocked off their hinges. He walked through the gap and came face to face with, not a castle, but a substantial house. He reasoned that whoever was the head of this village must have lived here.

The tramp could see more and more skeletons, and sea-shells were scattered everywhere.

The house was riddled with holes - it was like it had been shot at, and every window had been smashed. It now stood derelict. It was obvious to him that nobody had lived here for a long time.

The tramp walked towards the house until he came to the front doors. Surprisingly the old oak doors were still intact, although they showed the scars of a battle. One of the doors was partly open. Above the door was a name and date. The tramp was even more frightened of what it read, because he now knew that Captain Wirgoil was once a real person, and that the challenge must be some kind of infection. The inscription read:

Darridy House

built in the year of our lord 1660AD

Home of Christine and Captain Wirgoil

It could clearly be seen that Christine and Captain Wirgoil's names had been added at a later date. Everything was becoming more and more puzzling,

He had seen numerous graves in the church cemetery, and every one of them read that it was a Captain Wirgoil that had been buried there. He couldn't understand how there could be so many Captain Wirgoils.

There was the grave of a person that was buried in 1968 but this village had the appearance like nobody had lived here for hundreds of years. But there were those three shops and the inn which were selling produce. Nothing made any sense. The tramp knew that all the answers had to be at those shops and inn, but he was also interested in the big house, and thought that there could be somebody living here. On the front door was a door knocker in the shape of what appeared to be a devil like face. The tramp muttered, "What a horrible door knocker to choose for such lovely doors!" The tramp got hold of the knocker and banged it several times as hard as he could, and shouted at the top of his voice, "HELLO!- HELLO! Is anybody there?"

There wasn't any response, so the tramp pushed the door open just wide enough for him to get through. He was a bit concerned about entering the house, because of what he had seen already in the village and surrounds, but he worked up his courage and went inside.

He was immediately shocked. On the entrance wall were writings that were in capital letters and they appeared to be written in blood! The blood had dripped from the words like paint runs,

"Errrrrr," said the tramp. "Who would do such a thing?" The tramp slowly read the writings. They read:

CURSE YOU CAPTAIN WIRGOIL AND CHRISTINE WIRGOIL TOO

YOUR SOULS WILL NEVER REST UNTIL YOU FULFIL THE CHALLENGE LAID ONTO YOU, CHEATS. 1670

The same verse was written over and over again on all the walls.

"I wonder what that's about?" spoke the tramp talking aloud. "It was written a long time ago, sounds like some sort of pirate curse - I wonder what the challenge was? This sure is a horrible place. I'm surprised that it's all still here. Why haven't the police come here? It's definitely a murder scene, there's bodies everywhere, and look at all these threats that Captain and Christine Wirgoil had made to them, very odd - very odd," muttered the tramp.

He walked further into the house. Every room that he came to was the same, everything had been smashed to pieces and there was that verse everywhere. Although everything had been destroyed, it all looked remarkably fresh. All the furniture, paintings, crockery even bed linen had the look about them like all of this carnage had just happened, but the tramp knew that it must have happened hundreds of years ago. He felt like he was in some sort of time warp.

The tramp walked up the stairs; every step he took, the stair creaked. Strangely throughout the house were broken sea -shells, and as the tramp walked he was stepping on them.

He came to a room where the door was still intact. This was the first room that he had come to, where the door was still on its hinges. Every other door looked like it had been opened forcibly.

The door was closed and locked. The tramp tried to kick it open, but it wouldn't budge. He knocked on the door, not really expecting anybody to answer.

He shouted, "HELLO! HELLO! Is anybody in there?" But there wasn't, so the tramp decided to shoulder charge the door. He ran at the door using his right shoulder as a battering ram but the door held firm. The tramp rebounded off and fell to the floor in some pain. He rubbed his shoulder and muttered under his breath, "I won't be doing that again," or words to that effect.

He picked up an axe that happened to be handily lying on the floor, and hit the door with great fury. He was getting his own back at the door for hurting him. He hit the door over and over again with the axe but it didn't leave the slightest mark on it.

The tramp decided enough was enough. He realised that forces were working in this house that he didn't understand. He walked away muttering something. Suddenly and unexpectedly the door opened by itself. A puff of white smoke came out of the door as it opened, followed by a horrible smell, like that of a spoiled milk. The tramp held his nose with his fingers trying to mask the smell and entered the room. It was freezing cold inside which the tramp found very odd, it being a very warm day, and the rest of the house also warm. He looked around the room. Everything appeared to be untouched, everything was antique.

There was a rather nice carriage clock on a marble mantelpiece, and a ceramic washing bowl on a dressing table with women's items, including hair brushes and make -up. There was a mirror acting as a centre piece to the dressing table. The tramp looked into the mirror expecting to see his reflection but there was no reflection of him. It was as if he wasn't actually there. He walked away from the mirror and then walked back and peered at it, once again; the mirror showed no reflection of him. He picked up the hair brush and waved it from side to side in front of the mirror. The brush appeared but it looked like it was floating from side to side by itself. This amused the tramp but he knew that it was all very worrying and unexplainable. It was like magic.

In the room was a double bed and the bed linen was clean. The bed had the appearance like it had just been made. On each side of the bed were ornate bedside tables with drawers, and each table had a silver candle stick on it, with unused candles.

The tramp's eyes caught sight of a book. He thought that it was possibly a diary on one of the tables. He instinctively picked it up to read. Suddenly the bedroom door slammed shut with a mighty bang. This startled the tramp and made him drop the book to the floor. "Must be the wind," reasoned the tramp. He tried to open the door but it wouldn't budge. He could hear a voice coming from outside the room on the landing. He listened carefully to what the voice was saying.

"Leave - my - book - alone," is what he thought he heard.

"What?" shouted the tramp. "Who's there?"

"Christine, Christine, where are you? I'm sorry," said the voice.

The tramp shouted back, "I'm not going to touch your book. I don't like reading anyway, and there's no Christine in here, so can you let me out of this room? Who are you anyway? I wasn't doing any harm. I didn't think that there was anybody living in this house, what with the state of it and all. So if you let me out I'll go on my way."

The tramp picked the book up from the floor and placed it back on the bedside table. As he did this, the door violently swung open bashing the tramp on the back of his head.

"OUCH!" yelled the tramp. "I told you that I was going, there was no need for that."

The tramp turned towards the door to see who he had been talking to, but there was nobody there. He walked up and down the landing looking into each room but he couldn't see anybody.

This frightened the tramp. He ran towards the stairs as fast as he could. He wanted out of this place as quickly as possible. He made his way back down the steep steps and went back to the shops but they were all still closed, so he made his way to the church.

At the church he spotted a narrow path which he hadn't noticed before. Suddenly he could hear somebody calling, "Christine! - Christine, where are you?" The tramp looked around but he couldn't see anybody.

"Who's this Christine? There's a mention of a Christine Wirgoil on the walls of that house, but that was written hundreds of years ago, she wouldn't be around now," mumbled the tramp to himself.

The tramp stood where he was and shouted out, "Hello! I can hear you but I can't see you. Where are you? Show yourself. I'm sorry but I don't know anybody called Christine. In fact I haven't seen anybody in this place yet."

There wasn't any reply.

The tramp decided to explore the path. He walked for about five minutes and came to a rather beautiful sandy beach that led to the sea. The sea was very calm. Gentle waves came in accompanied by warm sea breezes. The air was fresh. The tramp felt good here. After his ordeal at the house this place seemed to be like heaven.

The tramp was rather the worse for wear by all the bashing he had taken in the last hour.

He decided to wash his hands and face in the sea water. He cupped the water in his hands and immediately dropped it. The water was just off freezing point!! The tramp stood there completely dumbfounded. His face grimaced. It was several minutes before he was able to speak.

"What on god's earth is going on here?" moaned the tramp. "How can this be?" he growled. The coldness of the water frightened him, because he knew that it would be impossible for him to be able to swim his way out of this village.

He didn't know where he was, and couldn't see any signs of life even down here by the sea. There wasn't anything - there's usually, always, sea birds squalling by the sea but not here. The tramp had thoughts that they should have called this place, " *The Village of the Dead!!"*

Out at sea, he could see a large rock formation that completely hid this place from anybody's view. He could see that it would be very treacherous to come into this bay unless you knew the way in. The rock formation looked like a small mountain range that was guarding this place.

The tramp could see that a ship had tried to come in but it had failed, because a mast had stuck out of the water. Surprisingly the flag of its country was still attached, and was fluttering in the warm sea breezes. The ensign was that of England and could only be seen when the tide was out.

The tramp was a bit surprised but everything that was happening was completely crazy.

He was standing on the beach looking around at his surroundings and was pondering as to what he was going to do. He knew that he was trapped here.

The tramp could hear his stomach rumbling which was the indication to him, that he really needed some food. He couldn't wait any longer and hoped that the shops would be open.

He put his hand in his pocket to search for small change. He could only find two, one shilling coins, six pennies and some other very low value coins. He knew that wasn't going to last him very long. He had to get some money from somewhere otherwise he wouldn't last long here.

Chapter Two: The Shell Man

He turned to go back to the village when suddenly he could see somebody walking toward him along the beach. This excited him. At last! he thought, a person.

The person was still a fair distance away from him but he could tell that it was a man, because he could see somebody with a very long beard and long hair. The man was carrying a bag. Every now and again he would stoop down and pick something up from the sandy beach.

The man was zig-zagging which left marks on the fresh damp sand.

As the man got nearer, the tramp could see that he was a rather dirty man, more like a tramp, but he didn't associate with anything like him, although for all intents and purposes he looked the same as this man.

He could now see what he was doing. He was meticulously picking up sea shells. Every now and again, he would get very angry and throw a shell away, moaning and groaning to himself.

The man was close to the tramp now but didn't seem to be noticing him - the tramp could hear the man counting, "One thousand two hundred and two- one thousand two hundred and three."

"Hello sir," spoke the tramp, politely. The man didn't take the slightest bit of notice of him.

"Hoi! Hoi! You. I'm talking to you, why don't you answer?"

The man ignored the tramp and walked past him, all the time counting those shells. They seemed to be very important to him.

This really annoyed the tramp. "Hoi, you, I'm talking to you. Why are you so rude? What are you doing? Why are you picking up those shells?"

The man stopped and turned round to face the tramp and growled at him.

"Because- just, because," was his vague reply, and then the man walked off.

Suddenly the most horrible smell that the tramp had ever smelt wafted up his nose. The tramp had to cough. "Wow! My God: you stink!" The tramp realised that the smell was coming from the shell man. The tramp fell to his knees on the sandy beach holding his nose. It looked like he was in great pain.

When the shell man was a reasonable distance away, the tramp let go of his nose, but he could now smell something that was nearly as bad - he realised that the second smell was coming from him! The tramp couldn't make head nor tail as to what was going on with the shell man but he was happy to see that there were people living here.

The tramp was now very, very hungry and thirsty. It was a warm humid day and he really needed something to eat and drink. He made his way back up the path towards the church and then went to the shops. He hadn't noticed that the church clock had changed its time. It now told the time as twelve noon. Suddenly there came the distinctive sound of clock chimes. The church clock that he thought wasn't working, chimed twelve times. On the last chime all the shops and inn opened their doors for business.

"At last!" rejoiced the tramp. "It's about time, it's a strange time for these shops to open unless it's half day opening or something, but at least they're open now, so I can get something to eat and drink."

The tramp walked to the baker's first - the smell of the freshly baked bread was too much for him to resist. He went into the baker's and was met by a very strange looking person. He didn't look anything like a baker. He didn't really even look like a real man.

The baker was wearing pirate clothing, and it was obvious that he was wearing a mask to hide his face. And he was wearing gloves. The tramp thought that was just for hygiene purposes but the gloves were rather dirty. The mask had a hideous smiley grin and appeared to be made out of paper mache. It had been painted a devil red colour. It had eyes painted on, but the tramp couldn't see any slots cut out so he couldn't figure out how it was possible for the baker to see. A rather large pointed nose had been moulded onto the face, which made it look ridiculous. It was also obvious that he was wearing a wig which was long, black and curly. The baker seemed to be very unstable; he was wobbling, and his body creaked as he moved.

"Afternoon sir, what can I get for you?" spoke the baker in a distinctive pirate accent.

"Baker, how much is your bread?" asked the tramp politely.

"Anything you like sir, as long as it's money," came the reply. Then the baker laughed but you couldn't see his mouth move, because it was a painted mouth with no holes.

"Anything I like? - that's odd," thought the tramp. "What's the price of bread today? I think that it's about one shilling. I don't know how long I'm going to be here, so I can't really afford that - I'll give him a penny and see what happens. I'm sure he'll be happy with that. After all, he hasn't got many customers - in fact, I'm the only one." The tramp was mumbling to himself.

He handed over a penny and laughed. He then asked for the largest loaf that the baker had, not really believing that he would get it. The baker handed him the bread and took the penny and said, "That'll be fine. Aye, fine sir."

The tramp walked out of the baker's with the largest loaf that was possible, but he really fancied a filling for the bread, so he made his way to the butcher's. He could see that it stocked a good range of cheeses as well as meat and poultry.

He was just about to go in when the shell man pushed past him and went into the shop first.

The butcher looked exactly like the baker, with the same type of mask and pirate clothing.

The shell man went up to the counter. The tramp stood behind him but he had to hold onto his nose, because of the smell. The butcher handed the shell man a bag of all sorts of meat and cheeses. And he asked him for gold. The tramp was shocked and wondered where the shell man would get gold from. The shell man handed the butcher a large bag. The butcher emptied the contents and counted every one of the gold pieces. But they weren't gold, they were sea shells.

"Thank you Captain. that'll be fine, aye fine," said the butcher. Then the shell man walked out of the shop with his bag of food but he didn't look very happy.

The tramp was bewildered. He had just seen the shell man give the butcher a bag of useless shells for his bag of lovely meat and cheeses, and the butcher believed the shells to be gold. Was everybody in this place bonkers?" thought the tramp. He followed the shell man into the baker's, and the same thing happened, and the baker also called the shell man "Captain".

The tramp thought that he would try the same ploy as the shell man, so he went back to the beach and picked up a few shells. And then made his way back to the butcher's laughing to himself.

"Hello butcher."

"Hello sir," replied the butcher, his gloved right hand dangling from his body.

Just like the baker he looked extremely thin.

"How much is that lovely piece of cheese?" asked the tramp, pointing to the largest piece of cheese in the shop.

"Anything you like sir, as long as it's money." replied the butcher, and then he laughed.

"Ok, Here's a piece of gold for the cheese butcher." The tramp handed the butcher the shell with a smug look on his face.

"No - no, sir don't be silly, that'll not be gold. That'll be a sea shell sir. I need money, aye money." and he handed the shell back to the tramp.

The tramp was a bit miffed. "Why can't you take this sea shell, oh, I mean; gold. You took it from the other man."

"Aye, sir that'll be right but he'll be the Captain and he always pays in gold, aye, gold."

"No! No! it wasn't gold, it was sea shells. I saw you counting them, and you told him that it would be fine, and they weren't gold, they were definitely ordinary sea shells. I saw him picking them up from the beach earlier on."

The butcher shook his head from side to side. Every time he did this, his head seemed to click, In fact every time he and the baker, earlier, moved their bodies you could hear rather strange clicking, and clunking noises.

"Ok then, if you want to play that game, I'll give you money." The tramp wasn't very happy about this.

"You say that I can give you anything, as long as it's money." The tramp pulled out a low value foreign coin from his pocket that he had found, and handed it to the butcher, not believing that he would take it.

The butcher took the coin, nodded his head in agreement that it was money and handed the tramp the cheese and told him that it would be fine. The tramp walked out of the butcher's wondering what on earth was going on here.

He walked over to an old iron bench and sat down and ate his cheese and bread. He could just about tell that where he was sitting was once the village green but there was nothing *green* about it now. Bones of people were lying all over the place, but the tramp was becoming used to it now, and didn't take any notice.

The tramp finished his bread and cheese and quite fancied a pint of beer, so he walked to the inn. He could smell the shell man, so he knew that he wouldn't be far away from here. The tramp walked into the inn. There wasn't anybody there except the barman, who looked exactly like the butcher and baker.

"Hello bartender, can you tell me something please, are the butcher and baker your brothers?"

"Aye sir, that'll be correct, aye, we're sort of brothers, you could say that, I suppose."

"Why do you wear masks, and why are you all dressed in pirate clothing?"

"Mask? No sir, I'll not be wearing a mask, and these are my normal clothes, aye, we're all normal here. What can I get you sir?"

"I could really down a pint of your best bitter barman." The tramp knew that he was wearing a mask but he thought, what's the point in arguing? It was obvious that all the people in this village were crazy. The barman poured the tramp a pint of some kind of beer in a battered metal tankard and handed it to him.

Like the butcher and baker his whole body was unstable. He could barely stand up.

"How much is that?" asked the tramp already expecting the answer.

"Anything you like sir, as long as it's money," and then the barman laughed.

The tramp handed the barman a penny and then laughed himself at giving the barman such a small amount of money for the beer.

"Aye that'll be fine sir, fine," said the barman, falling over backwards onto the floor. He struggled to get back to his feet.

The tramp didn't say anything; he thought that the barman was drunk.

The tramp sat down on an old wooden bench and put his beer on an old wooden table.

There were several skulls propped up on the bar, and everyone was looking at him. The tramp stared at the skulls and wondered who these people once were. He finished his pint and quite fancied another although it didn't taste very good. He walked up to the barman and asked for the same. He didn't bother to ask how much. He just handed the barman a penny. Which he accepted.

While the tramp was sitting there drinking his beer it was becoming noticeable that there was a pong in the air and it was coming his way. The reason for the smell walked in the door; it was the shell man. He walked to the bar, and suddenly all the skulls moved, and were now facing the shell man. The barman handed the shell man a pint of beer. "Here Captain, here's your ale. You need to pay now sir. I'll have your gold if you don't mind." The shell man handed the barman a bag of something. All the time he was moaning something about the cost of his beer. The barman poured the contents of the bag on the counter and counted the shells.

The tramp didn't know why the shell man was complaining about getting beer for sea shells. It seemed to be a bit of a bargain to him. The barman thanked him, and then the shell man sat down close to the tramp. The tramp nodded his head in amazement at what he was witnessing. It hadn't worked for him, but the shell man seemed to be getting away with it.

The shell man was sitting at the next table to the tramp. The tramp couldn't face him, because of the smell. He quickly finished his pint and got up to leave. As he left, he noticed that all the skulls that were on the bar, were now on the shell man's table and he appeared to be talking to them.

The tramp fancied some fruit, so he made his way into the greengrocer's. The greengrocer, as expected by the tramp looked exactly like the butcher, baker and bartender.

"Hello, greengrocer."

"Afternoon sir, what can I do for you?" said the greengrocer.

The greengrocer's rickety body was swaying from side to side, he seemed to be very unstable.

"Could I have some apples please - the biggest ones that you've got?" asked the tramp.

"Certainly, sir. Nice afternoon for it, isn't it?" said the greengrocer nodding his head up and down. His head was clicking like crazy.

"Nice afternoon for what?" asked the tramp looking at the greengrocer thinking that this man's head would fall off if he kept nodding.

"Nothing particular," said he. His head was now tilting to one side. The greengrocer tried to rectify it by bashing his head with his hand, but his hand seemed to fall off!!

The greengrocer bent down, when he got back up his gloved hand was attached.

The tramp laughed. "Did your hand just fall off?"

"No, no, no, it's just my party trick sir - it's good isn't it?"

"Yeah, it's very good, too good, I think," said the tramp to himself.

"Can I have my apples now, please?"

"Certainly sir, here be your apples."

"How much are they? Don't tell me, anything I like, as long as it's money."

"Aye that'll be right, sir."

The tramp delved into his pocket looking for anything that would be considered as money. He found a farthing (a British coin of very little value that was out of circulation) and he handed it to him.

The grocer nodded his head. He seemed to know that it was money.

"Thank you sir, that'll be fine, aye fine."

The tramp walked out of the greengrocer's thinking that he was in some kind of loony place, everything was pretty strange.

He went back to the bench. As he walked, he was stepping on broken sea shells that were scattered everywhere. He wondered why he had bothered to go to the beach to get his shells, but the shells in the village were only small fragments, and the shell man's shells that he gave for his food and drink appeared to be whole shells.

The tramp had just finished his last apple when the church clock chimed again - it chimed once, so it was 1 pm according to that clock. Instantly all the shops and inn closed.

The tramp was now very tired and fell fast asleep on the bench. He slept for hours, and when he woke up he looked at his pocket watch. It was now 6:16 pm but the pocket watch had stopped so the tramp had no idea now as to what the actual time was. All the shops and the inn were still closed. There would be no way now for the tramp to ever calibrate his watch again.

He could see the shell man approaching him, and he had a rather angry look on his face. He came stomping up to the tramp, carrying a stick in his hand, and was moaning and groaning.

"Where's my shells?" he yelled.

"What!" the tramp was startled.

"Where's - my - shells?" repeated the shell man, with a frown on his face.

"What shells?" replied the tramp, looking baffled.

"The ones that you've stolen, they're in your pocket, I can see them. Give them to me, they're mine. All the shells here are mine. I'm three shells short. I won't be able to get any more food and drink unless I pay what I owe. So give them to me now, before I hit you with this stick."

"Oh," said the tramp, "I didn't know that you could own shells off a beach. Here you are, you can have them, they're no good to me, but the shop keepers and barman think that they're gold when you give them to them. How come?"

"Because, I'm the Captain, that's why."

"Captain?"

"Yeah, Captain. Well that's what they call me, I don't know why."

"Captain of what? Have you got a ship?" asked the tramp sarcastically.

"No, I haven't got a ship. I accepted the..." The shell man couldn't say the word *challenge*. "Yeah, that's what I did, I accepted the...." Once again he was not able to say the word.

The shell man looked down at the ground with a look of hopelessness on his face.

"What's the challenge?" The tramp guessed that's what the shell man was trying to say.

"I've seen a lot of people buried in the cemetery that had all died of the challenge. Can you tell me what it is? Is it a disease?"

"No!" replied the shell- man. "I can't tell you, you have to find out for yourself."

"But I don't want to find out," moaned the tramp. "I want to get out of this crazy place - how do I get out?"

"There's no way out, unless you accept the ...you know what," said the shell man despairingly.

The tramp shook his head and muttered something under his breath.

"Go to the church. She'll tell you."

"Who will tell me?"

"Christine, that's who, she'll tell you," and then the shell man walked off with the three shells in his hand that the tramp had taken from the beach. He seemed to wobble a bit as the beer had taken effect.

The tramp had no choice but to make his way to the church he had to find out who this Christine was, and what this challenge was. The tramp came to the two big arched oak church doors but they were still locked, so he banged on them and shouted out, "Christine! Christine! I have to talk to you. It's about the challenge. The shell man said that you knew something about it. I have to know what it is. The shell man said that I wouldn't be able to get out of this place unless I accepted the challenge, and I really don't want to stay here, everybody is, well, pretty barmy!!"

Chapter Three: The Challenge

Suddenly the oak doors of the church slowly creaked open. The tramp could see what appeared to be a woman, but he wasn't sure - she was wearing very old fashion clothing, something that women of the 17th century would wear. She was wearing a mask but it wasn't like the others'. It was something resembling a woman's face but a very ugly one. It was painted a devil red colour, and once again it had painted eyes and mouth but no slots were cut out so she surely couldn't see anything.

The woman stood face to face with the tramp. Her dress was very long and beautiful but a bit ragged. She was wearing dirty white gloves that completely covered her very thin arms. She, too, was obviously wearing a long curly wig, but her wig was blond.

"Hello, young man," spoke the woman in a posh London accent. Her voice was remarkably clear considering that the mask covered her mouth, "I've been expecting you."

"Expecting me ma'am? How did you know that I was coming? I didn't even know, myself. Why is everybody here wearing a mask? And what is this place? It feels like everybody is dead here, except the stinking shell man, and he's bonkers! He's collecting sea shells and those stupid shop keepers think that the sea shells are gold. Everybody is nuts here, and who and what are you?"

"I'm Christine, you've been asking for me." She spoke softly.

"Well yes, I have. I want to get out of this place but the shell man says the only way out is to accept the challenge but I don't know what the challenge is."

The tramp scratched his head in frustration at the question.

"The shell man didn't actually say the word challenge, ma'am, but I guessed that's what he was trying to say. Is that right?"

"Yes, that's right, the only way out is to accept the challenge," said Christine. Her body was jerking uncontrollably as she spoke.

The tramp's face dropped. "But you can't keep me a prisoner here. It's against the law."

"There's no law here," said Christine. "We rule ourselves. Have done for a long time.

There is a way out though, so you're not really a prisoner, and I could make you very wealthy."

The tramp's eyes lit up at the word "wealthy"; that's what he'd wanted all his life. He wanted to be rich. That was the most important thing in his whole existence.

"Wealthy, ma'am? How?" were the last three words to come out of his dribbling mouth.

"You have to accept the challenge," said Christine.

"What's the challenge? And what happens if I don't accept this challenge?"

The tramp had a broad smile on his face; his mind was focusing on the wealth.

"You'll surely die of starvation sir," said Christine, calmly.

"Oh!" said the tramp "That's not good. What is the challenge?"

Christine read out the terms and conditions of the challenge that were written on an old document. They were as follows:

THE CHALLENGE

You are challenged to collect 10 sacks of 1000 shells - each shell has to be perfect.

You're allowed to collect 1210 shells per month. All your food and drink has to be paid for with shells. At the start of the challenge you have to pay all the first month's bills in full. Thereafter you pay at the end of each month. You must pay the butcher, baker, greengrocer and the Inn keeper the same amount asked for by the challenge regardless of what you have had from them. You will only have to pay each of them one sea shell for the first month's food and drink bill. At the end of the second month the cost will go up to two shells to each of them. Each month thereafter the price will double until you have fulfilled the challenge.

Be warned, if at the end of the first year you haven't fulfilled the challenge.

The challenge will begin again on the first day of June but you pay the bill at the end of June. If on the last day of that month you haven't paid all your bills in full, you will no longer be able to get any food and drink, and so would have failed the challenge.

The person who fulfils the challenge will be rewarded with all treasures belonging to Captain Nigel Wirgoil

Instigated on the last day of May 1670 by the last remaining crew members of Captain Nigel Wirgoil

The tramp stood there thinking about the challenge. It seemed so easy and the thought of being paid to do it, seemed to him ridiculous, and he could get all the food and drink that he required for nothing, barring a few worthless sea shells. He thought about this before making a firm decision.

"Now let me think, um..." The tramp was thinking and talking aloud, "...I can collect 1210 shells every month, and I can get all the food and drink that I want for a whole month for only one shell to each of the shops and the inn. That's four shells for the first month, and it will be eight shells for the next month.

In those two months I will have collected 2420 shells, and only have to pay out 12 shells.

This seems to be so easy, what a bit of luck - I don't have any choice. I will starve to death here anyway if I don't accept the challenge, because I haven't got much real money left".

"Christine," he said.

"Yes." Christine was now wobbling so much that she was in danger of falling over.

"It sounds good to me but I'm not going to rush into it. I want to see the wealth that I will receive if I fulfil this challenge, first, before I accept."

"Of course you do," said Christine, "follow me."

Christine turned around. Her body was clunking even more as she did this movement. It seemed hard for her to turn her body.

She led the tramp. Suddenly a thick mist sprung up from nowhere. The tramp had no idea as to where Christine was taking him. She walked very slowly.

The tramp was hanging onto Christine's dress for guidance. About ten minutes passed. The mist dispersed, and the tramp found himself in a cave where there were old metal caskets. A chain had been put around them which connected them all together. The tramp could see eight caskets but it was dim in the cave and he didn't know if that was all of them. A cover was over something. The tramp didn't know what it was but he thought that it could be more caskets.

Christine told the tramp to open one of the caskets. The tramp walked to one of them and prised the lid open.

"There you are young man, there's your wealth - this will be your prize if you fulfil the challenge."

The tramp stood there with his mouth wide open in shock. The casket was full to the brim with gold coins, jewellery of the finest quality - this one casket alone would be worth millions of pounds, and there were at least seven other caskets.

The tramp could barely speak. "Do I only get um, this um - this um…" He couldn't get the words out of his mouth "…one casket, Christine?"

"No, they're all yours."

The tramp laughed out loud. It was a hideous, greedy kind of laugh.

"Mine!! All mine!! How many caskets are there?"

"Ten," replied Christine.

"Ten!" The tramp again laughed out loud and fell to the ground crying with uncontrollable emotion.

After a few minutes he got up to his feet and started dancing around all the other caskets. He was opening them one by one. Every time he opened another casket he went into an uncontrollable hysterical laughing fit.

The tramp was becoming delirious with treasure fever. He started talking to himself.

"I'm the luckiest man in the whole world, who would have thought it? *Me*, a rich man? But didn't I always say that I would be rich! Yes I did. I told Albert that I wanted to be rich. I wish Albert was here now to see this. The challenge is easy, so I might as well say that I'm a rich man already."

"I can't wait to start this challenge. I know that it will take a few months but I'm going to be well cared for. Now, um, let me see, what shall I do? I'm going to make sure that this really is my treasure, Christine."

"Yes," Christine's head had fallen onto her chest - she seemed to find it hard to lift her head back up.

"Well, yes, yes, I really like the sound of the challenge but could you tell me why it is so easy?"

"Because we want you to win," came her reply.

The tramp liked her answer. "Oh, I see, but who is "we?"

"My husband - he's here. If you complete the challenge, we'll all be able to leave this place. We're trapped here too."

"Oh dear, yeah, I can understand that. So I'm helping you then?" The tramp had calmed down now.

"Yes, you could say that," Christine didn't sound that convincing though.

"But why doesn't your husband take up the challenge?" asked the tramp still grinning with the excitement of seeing the treasure.

"Because he's not allowed to," said Christine sadly.

"Oh, ok then, I don't see anything wrong so I will accept the challenge but I want a signed document to say that all, and I mean all!! of the treasure will be mine once I complete the challenge, which of course, I will do."

"Of course you do," said Christine, "I have the document right here for you to sign. I've signed it already."

She handed the tramp the document and a very old nib ink pen which would have been used hundreds of years ago. Her gloved hand moved very slowly and clunked as she handed it to him. The pen nib didn't appear to be holding any ink. The tramp couldn't see how it could possibly write anything but he pressed it onto the old paper and surprisingly it did write his name.

Chapter Four: Accepting The Challenge

The tramp's hands were trembling with excitement but he was careful to read the document's terms and conditions that Christine had already read out to him, and agreed with them before he signed it.

"Thank you Captain, and good luck," said Christine. Her gloved hand clicked as she took the document back from the tramp.

"A- What? - Captain? No, I'm not a Captain," said the tramp shaking his head from side to side. "No, not me, absolutely not."

The tramp was clearly annoyed at being called Captain.

"Follow me," Christine led the tramp. The mist that had accompanied them to this place rose up again from nowhere so the tramp had no idea as to where the treasure was.

Christine led the tramp back to the church and then the mist dispersed.

The tramp was puzzled by something. "Christine, why doesn't it ever get dark here?"

"Because we're caught in a time warp. Always will be until the challenge has been completed."

"You know, that's what I thought. I knew that this place was something very odd."

The tramp was beginning to get a bit worried when Christine called him "Captain." Alarm bells were ringing in his head. He'd seen all the graves in the cemetery with the name of Captain Wirgoil inscribed on all of them, and now, he was being called Captain.

"Can I ask you something Christine, how long has this challenge been going on?"

She paused for quite a while; it was like she didn't want to answer the question.

"Since 1670," she told him.

"What? 1670?" The tramp was shocked. "But it's now 1969. The challenge is easy. Why hasn't anybody been able to complete it in nearly three hundred years? It doesn't make sense."

"That you must find out for yourself, Captain." Christine sounded very sad.

The tramp had signed the document, so he was now committed to the challenge. He wouldn't be able to get out of it. There wouldn't be any point either - he had very little money, and there was no way out of this place.

The tramp suddenly became aware that Christine had disappeared - she seemed to have vanished into thin air. The tramp had another question for her. He wanted to find out more about Captain Wirgoil.

The tramp slowly realised that the shell man had in his own way already told him that he was doing the challenge. This made him very angry. He stormed off down to the beach to have it out with him. He started walking very quickly, nearly running. All the time he was ranting to himself.

"He's not getting my treasure, nobody is, it's all mine, and I'm not sharing it with anyone," he told himself in no uncertain terms.

When he got to the beach there was no sign of the shell man. The tramp decided that there wasn't a minute to lose, so he thought that he would start collecting shells immediately.

"I'm going to collect more than what she says - I'll work harder. If I can get say, 2000, or maybe even more shells in a month, I'll fulfil the challenge quicker, and I'll be able to get out of this place. Maybe I can get the ten thousand shells in a few weeks. Who's to stop me? The challenge is to collect ten thousand shells, so when I get them, the treasure will be mine. She doesn't realise how clever I am." He felt very pleased with himself.

"But I can't understand why the shell man is collecting - I've signed a contract to say that all the treasure will be mine, and I'm certainly not going to share my wealth with that dirty shell man. I can't see him but I can sure smell him. He's around here somewhere. Oh, the tide's coming in too fast for me to be able to collect any shells so I might as well take a nap. I'll start collecting later."

The tramp walked back to the village green and slept on the bench. When he woke up, he glanced at the church clock.

"Oh, I've slept for hours - it's 12.42. The shops and the inn are open. It must be the next day. There's no sense of time in this place. I didn't hear the clock chimes and I haven't collected any shells. I'm hungry. I'll go to the shops first and get something to eat - I'll get some shells later on, I haven't got much time."

The tramp was talking to himself. He was already going a bit mad being in this place. He walked over towards the shops.

He walked into the baker's and was greeted with, "Morning Captain, here's your bread and cakes. Is there anything else?"

"Captain? What you calling me 'captain' for? I'm not a Captain - I've never even been in a boat, I don't know what you're on about. How much is the bread and cakes - don't tell me anything I like as long as it's money."

"No Captain, that'll not be right - no money sir, you have to pay in gold, aye, gold."

"Oh God," the tramp thought, "I forgot the terms of the challenge. They said that I have to pay for the first month's goods with a sea shell at each shop and pay at the end of the month thereafter. I need to find a sea shell but I wonder if the baker will take cash money. There's no harm in trying."

"Baker, I don't have any gold at the moment. I haven't started collecting yet. Here's a penny for the bread and cakes, how's that?"

"No good, Captain - it has to be gold, aye gold."

"But I don't have any gold - what about if I give you your gold tomorrow?" The tramp nodded his head expecting the baker to agree with his proposition.

"Sorry Captain, that won't do, it has to be gold. I can't give you any food unless you give me the gold."

"But I don't have any gold, and I'm really hungry. I'll tell you what I'll do; I'll give you all the money that I have – here's a shilling. How's that?" The tramp stood there expecting the answer to be 'yes'.

"No, Captain, it has to be gold, aye gold."

The tramp walked out of the baker's in a huff and ran to the beach as fast as he could to collect some shells. But the tide was in, so it wasn't possible to collect any. He knew that the shell man had probably been into the shops already, because he could smell that he'd been in the baker's.

The tramp walked along the beach using his nose as a guide to find the shell man. The smell started to get stronger and stronger. His nose told him that the shell man was behind a rock just a few yards away from where he was now standing. He held his nose and walked to the rock and confronted the shell man.

"I say, it's a nice day, isn't it?" said the tramp trying to be nice to him.

"It's always a nice day here. What do you want?" The shell man growled at him.

"That's a rather nice Cornish pasty that you're eating, would you like to share it with me? I'm sorry to bother you but the baker wouldn't give me any food unless I gave him a piece of gold, which as you know, is a sea shell. But I haven't got any, and the tide is in, so I won't be able to get any. And I'm really hungry. Please give me a piece of your pasty, a little piece will do."

The tramp was reduced to begging.

"Push off! You'll not be getting any of my food, it's all mine," said the shell man abruptly.

"Blimey!" said the tramp. "I only asked, you don't have to take that sort of attitude. If it was me, I would have shared with you. What about lending me a shell then?"

"Go away! Hop it," said the shell man.

"Alright, I'm going, I'll find my own shell. I can see one over there by that rock. That'll do for a start. I'll get a pie with that."

"Leave my shells alone," shouted the shell man. "That shell is mine, it's on my land. You're not allowed to take shells from my land."

"His land? I wonder what he means by that? I really need a shell. I haven't got much time left before the baker shuts. I'll walk back towards the shops, I might find one on the way.

That man is bonkers. What a greedy person! He wouldn't even give me a piece of his pie. I'll get my own back at him one day."

The tramp made his way back towards the shops. He'd forgotten that he was going to confront the shell man about the challenge. Hunger, not the treasure, was his main thought at this moment in time. When he was nearly back to the pathway he spotted a sea shell but it was on top of quite a steep rock. The tramp was now so hungry that he would do anything for a shell.

That shell was equivalent to a piece of gold at this moment, to the tramp.

He started climbing up the rock in a attempt to get the shell but it was too sheer and slippery and the tramp fell off and came down to earth with a bit of a bang. He didn't let that put him off though. He was determined to get that shell, and after several attempts he finally managed to grab hold of it, but to his horror there was a very small chip in the shell. The terms of the challenge had stated that the shells had to be perfect but it was a very tiny chip, hardly noticeable. Maybe the baker wouldn't notice it, hoped the tramp, and if the baker said anything he would explain to him that was all he could find. He was sure that the baker would understand.

He ran as fast as he could to the bakers - he was really gasping for breath when he reached it. There was only about a minute to go before the shops shut.

"Hello, baker. Well, I've got your piece of gold that you asked for, and I can tell you that it was hard for me to get, so can I have some food now please? I'm starving!"

"Aye you can, Captain - that'll be one piece of gold, please." The baker held out his gloved hand for the shell.

"Here's your gold." The tramp proudly handed the baker the shell, really hoping that he wouldn't notice the small chip. He kept his hand covering it as he handed it to him.

"No, no, no Captain, that'll not do, you know the rules - that'll not be gold, that'll be a sea shell, aye, sea shell."

"No, it's gold," shouted the tramp in desperation.

"No, Captain, you can't get any food with a sea shell."

"No, it's gold, it's not a sea shell. Please, baker, I'm starving - I'll give you a piece of gold tomorrow, I promise."

"No gold, no food, Captain, they'll be the rules, aye, rules, you have to abide by the rules."

Suddenly the church clock chimed one.

"Closing time, Captain, I'll see thee tomorrow." The baker ushered out the tramp and locked the door.

The tramp was now outside the baker's, moaning and groaning. He was really in a bad mood now. He walked back to the beach. He knew that the shell man had some food. The tramp was desperate to get something to eat, so he worked out a plan to sneak up on the shell man and to steal some of his food while he was asleep.

He knew that the shell man was behind a rock, so he got as close to him as he could, and then went onto his hands and knees and slowly crawled towards him, like an animal stalking its prey.

The tramp could hear the shell man talking to himself, so he knew that he would have to bide his time. As he was waiting for the shell man to fall to sleep he could smell the Cornish pasty, and it was driving him mad. His stomach was rumbling, it was screaming for food.

The tramp sat there for over an hour. At last the shell man fell asleep - he could hear him snoring.

The tramp slowly crawled nearer and nearer to the rock - he was careful not to make a noise.

He was almost there, but the smell from the shell man was mingling with the smell from the pasty - the tramp tried to ignore the smell from the shell man in favour of the smell from the pasty, but it was in vain, because in the end the shell man's smell overwhelmed the smell from the pasty.

The air was now filled with stinking body odour. The tramp poked his head around the rock and could see the shell man fast asleep. There was a half- eaten Cornish pasty inches away from the shell man's filthy, dirty hand. The tramp licked his lips in anticipation of his meal. He slowly stretched his hand ever nearer the piece of pasty. He got his hand to it, and was just about to grab it when the smell of the shell man completely overwhelmed him. He had no choice but to cough. Which woke up the shell man.

"What do you think you're doing?" he yelled. "Get- off -my- land - you thief! Get your filthy hands off my pasty."

The tramp jumped up and yelled, "You're mental! What's wrong with you? I only want a bite out of your pasty. I'm hungry! It wouldn't hurt you to give me a piece."

"Push off!" said the shell man waving his stick.

"Don't bother anyway, the tide's going out now, so I can get my own shells - I won't go hungry again. And if you ever want anything from me, don't bother to ask, because I won't be helping you."

The tramp walked away and saw his first sea shell. He ran towards it like a man possessed. He tried to pull it out of the sand but it wouldn't budge. So he went to another, and another but it was the same story, they were all stuck tight in the sand.

Suddenly the shell man shouted, "Hoi, you tramp! You can't get any shells from my land, you can only collect them from your land."

"Who's he calling 'tramp'? Look at the state of him? Hoi, you, don't call me tramp, you're dirtier than I am, and you stink!"

"Well, so do you stink," ranted the shell man.

The tramp shouted, "So where's my land then?"

"You'll have to find out for yourself," shouted back the shell man.

Suddenly the tramp remembered why he wanted to confront the shell man.

"What are you doing anyway, collecting those shells? You can't be after the treasure, because it's going to be mine. I've signed a contract with Christine who's its guardian. When I've fulfilled the challenge it'll all be mine," boasted the tramp.

The shell man laughed. He tried to tell the tramp something but he couldn't get the words out of his mouth. It was like he was being gagged.

The tramp knew that he wasn't going to get anything from the shell man so he walked away from him. As he was walking, he could see what looked like a pile of rags over near the cliff face. He walked over to them and realised that it was a pile of sacks - ten in all. He guessed that these sacks were for him to collect the ten sacks of 1000 shells. Near the sacks, he could see a sea shell- he picked it up, and it was a whole one - the tramp was overjoyed. It was his first sea shell, and it wasn't stuck in the sand.

"So this must be my land," reasoned the tramp.

He started jumping up and down screaming, "I've got a shell! - I've got a shell!" He was like a child with a new toy. The tramp was so excited that he started running along the beach picking up all the shells like they were pieces of gold.

"One - two -three - four -five. I've got five already," he shouted.

Soon he had a handful, and couldn't carry anymore - he needed a bag. The shell man had a bag. The tramp wondered where he had got it from. He thought that there must be one around here somewhere. The sacks would become too heavy to cart around, and he had to make sure that he didn't break any of the shells.

He walked back to where the sacks were and lying behind them was what he was looking for. A nice cloth bag to collect the shells in. He was so enthralled at what he was doing, that he had forgotten about his hunger - collecting the shells had become more important.

He was going merrily about his business collecting the shells and he was singing:

"When I'm a rich man, I'm going to buy, buy, buy, buy, buy me
a big, big, big, big, big house in the country,
la, la ,la, la, la, la , la,
When I'm a rich man, I'm going to buy, buy, buy, buy, buy me
A big, big, big, big, big car
la, la, la, la, la, la, la"

The tramp carried on collecting the shells for nearly an hour and had amassed 47 shells when suddenly he went to pick one up and it was stuck tight in the sand - he couldn't force it, because it would break and be of no use. He tried several others but they were all stuck. He couldn't understand what was going on. He could see the shell man in the distance, and it looked like he had stopped collecting too.

There appeared to be some sort of limit as to how many shells you could collect at any one time. All that he knew was that he would be able to collect 1210 shells in a month but there was no sense of time here so he wouldn't know what days he would be allowed to collect shells. Tracking of time in this place would be impossible.

The tramp was very tired now anyway, so he walked back to where the sacks were. He wasn't sure where he was supposed to sleep. But he noticed a small cave, so he wandered inside - it was clear that people had used this cave before. There was a straw bed and cooking utensils, a wood burning stove was in a corner, but there was only one log to put into the stove.

There seemed to be everything that he would require to survive here.

The tramp was hungry, but happy. He'd started the challenge. He'd already got 47 shells. He only needed another 9953 and he would be a rich man. The tramp lay on the bed and fell fast asleep. He woke up the next day and everything was exactly the same. The sun was still shining - it was in the same place in the sky. It hadn't moved, and it was hot here. He could see that the tide had come and gone - there were loads of new sea shells, so he wasted no time. He collected another 32 shells when suddenly the same thing happened. The shells became stuck tight in the sand. It was like somebody was playing a game with him.

The tramp had thought that he would be able to collect more than the challenge had stated, but he now knew that it wouldn't be possible to collect more than 1210 shells in a month. So it didn't really matter how many shells he collected in a day, as long as he got his full quota by the end of the month.

The tramp was now very, very hungry. He'd gone a long time without food and drink but he knew that when the shops and inn opened he would be able to buy some food and drink with his sea shells. He knew that yesterday, if it was yesterday.

Because he had no sense of time in this place. The shops opened at twelve noon, church clock time. He had absolutely no idea what the real time was, or even what day it was. He decided to go for a walk and explore the village a bit more. He was worried about the shell man stealing his shells.

He started talking to himself, "Now then, where shall I put my gold? Oh, what's the matter with me? They're not gold, they're sea shells - I'm going mad here already and I've only been here for one day. Or is it two days? I don't know. I'm not going to get as dirty as that stinking shell man. He called me a tramp yesterday. I can't wash, because the water is too cold, and I haven't got a razor, so I can't shave. If I had some drinking water I suppose I could wash but I haven't got any - maybe I'll wash later on."

The tramp hid his shells and walked towards the church where the path to the village was.

The tramp wasn't really going to explore the village. He was trying to see if he could find the location of the treasure. He knew that he was taken to a cave of sorts. He searched everywhere, but he couldn't find the slightest clue as to where he had been taken. He walked back to the old church. The clock's hands were where they always were, stuck on 1:13. He went to the church front entrance trying to get in, because he knew that Christine had come from there. The oak doors were still locked. He wandered around the church looking all the time for any clue of an opening but he found nothing. He didn't want to go to the grave yard because it worried him. There were so many Captain Wirgoils buried there, and now he was being called Captain - he was hoping that he wouldn't be the next person to die of the challenge but he couldn't see why that should be.

He walked to the village bench and sat there thinking about things. He could see that this village was once a nice place but something had happened here that was really horrible. The skulls that were everywhere were an unnerving experience. They always appeared to be looking at him.

The tramp walked down the path towards the cottages and looked inside some of them, He could have lived in one of them but they were so creepy that he thought it better to live on the beach. There were things inside the cottages that could have been useful for him but if he tried to take anything from any of them he would be stopped. Nothing could be taken out of the cottages.

He could see another row of shops - there was once a tailor shop, and a hardware shop - and other shops but he couldn't make out what they once were. The ground was a mixture of sand and a red colour. It looked very much like dried blood. It never rained in this place, so that's probably what it was. The tramp didn't like this place and vowed never to come here again.

The church clock chimed twelve times, this indicated food and drink time. The tramp had already prepared himself for this and had put some whole sea shells in his pocket. The challenge document had said that he would only have to pay one shell to each of the three shops and the inn to get his food and drink. He went into the baker's first - the smell of the bread always seemed to draw him here.

The baker was standing at the counter.

"'Morning, Captain. Here's your bag of food, would there be anything else?" said the baker shaking uncontrollably.

"I'm not a Captain," said the tramp. He didn't like the word "Captain." Every Captain that he had heard of in this village was a dead Captain, except the shell man.

"I don't know why you call me Captain," said the tramp, "because I don't want to be Captain, so don't call me that again."

The baker didn't answer.

"What's in the bag anyway?"

"It's your allowed provisions Captain. You're only allowed a certain amount, plus one other item which can be your choice. What would you like?"

The tramp looked inside the bag to see what he had got.

He had a loaf of bread, and two cakes.

"I would like a hot Cornish pasty, please."

"Certainly, Captain." The baker handed the tramp the Cornish pasty.

"That'll be one piece of gold please, aye, one piece of gold."

The tramp proudly handed the baker a sea shell.

"That'll be fine, Captain, see thee tomorrow."

The tramp couldn't wait to eat the Cornish pasty, so he went over to the bench and sat there and ate it. He finished it very quickly.

He went into the butcher's next.

"Hello Captain, here's your meat, would you like anything else?" said the butcher who was also shaking violently.

"Yeah, I would like something else. Don't- call -me- Captain!" demanded the tramp.

The tramp looked in the bag to see what he had been given. He had a very small piece of beef. "Have you got any pork sausages, butcher?"

"Aye, Captain, that I have." The butcher handed the tramp three pork sausages.

"Is that all?" said the tramp puffing out a breath of air as a gesture of disappointment.

"Aye, Captain, that'll be all you're allowed. That'll be one piece of gold, aye one piece of gold."

The tramp handed the butcher the sea shell. Once again he felt very proud to do this.

"That'll be fine Captain. Aye fine."

"But how do I cook the sausages? There's only one log - that won't last long." moaned the tramp.

"The log will last as long as you," replied the butcher.

"Oh, that's good - an everlasting burning log, who would believe it?"

The tramp walked straight into the grocer's.

"Hello Captain, here be your groceries. Is there anything else?" The grocer's body was leaning to one side.

"Yeah, don't call me Captain!" The tramp looked in the bag. He had four potatoes, half a cabbage, a bottle of water, and some pig fat. Can I have some razor blades?"

"What be razor blades, Captain?"

"Oh, wrong era of time for razor blades," thought the tramp. "Can I have some soap?"

"No soup here Captain."

"No I said soap - not soup. You know the stuff that you wash yourself with. Oh, never mind. Give me a bag of apples then."

The grocer handed the tramp two apples.

"Is that all? I asked for a bag full."

"That's all you be allowed captain. That'll be one piece of gold."

The tramp handed the grocer a sea shell with a smug look on his dirty face.

"That'll be fine, aye, fine," said the grocer.

The tramp really fancied a pint of beer, so he went to the inn.

"Morning Captain, here be your pint of ale- is there anything else?" asked the bartender.

He appeared to have a leg missing.

"Yeah, don't call me Captain! And where's your leg?"

The bartender shuffled something under the counter.

"What do you mean, where's my leg? It's right here," the bartender pointed to his very thin legs and he did now have two.

"Oh, never mind, just give me another beer or whatever it is that you're serving."

"That'll be fine." The barman gave the tramp another pint of ale.

"That'll be one piece of gold please, aye, one piece of gold."

The tramp handed the barman a sea shell.

"That'll be fine, aye, fine." said the barman, limping.

"Are you people all crazy? It's not gold - it's a sea shell, and why do you keep repeating yourself? What's all this 'aye'? and that'll be fine? and 'aye' gold? It's getting boring, can't you stop saying that? Why don't you speak proper like me?" said the tramp

The barman didn't answer.

As the tramp walked back towards the beach the shell man was walking towards the baker's and went inside. The tramp followed him in just to see what happened.

"Hello Captain, here's your bag. Would you like anything else?" asked the baker.

"Meat pie," said the shell man, rather abruptly.

"Here you are, that's fine." The baker gave the shell man a meat pie.

"He's called him Captain too, and he didn't ask him for any gold. Oh, I remember now, he paid yesterday, which was the end of the month, so next time I have to pay, it will be the end of July - the shell man will have to pay at the end of June. I'll only have to pay two shells to each of them, so that won't be too bad. I'll have thousands of shells by then.

The tramp still hadn't realised the terms of the challenge regarding the shell man. He seemed oblivious to the fact that the shell man still being here in June doing the challenge - there must be something wrong. The shell man went to every shop except the greengrocer's, and then had a few pints of ale at the inn.

The tramp sat on the bench and waited for him. The shell man eventually walked towards him.

"Hoi, shell man. I'm, um, a bit baffled as to what is going on here. There's obviously been a battle fought here, looks like, by pirates. Would you happen to know anything about things?"

"No," said the shell man as he walked straight past the tramp without looking at him.

What a rude man! thought the tramp.

*

The weeks passed, the tramp had no idea of time. It was only when it came to paying his bills that he knew that it was the end of the month, or he was told that's what it was. The tramp paid his bills at the end of July but he noticed that the shell man was missing. He hadn't seen him around for quite a long time. But he wasn't too bothered about that, because the shell man wasn't very good company. He wandered down to what was the shell man's land, but he wasn't there, nothing was there. It was as if the shell man had vanished.

The tramp was really worried that the shell man had fulfilled the challenge and had got all the treasure. He was annoyed and ran as fast as he could to the church in search of Christine, who he hadn't seen since he signed the challenge document. He stood at the entrance to the front of the church, which was locked and he started banging on the door and shouting, "Christine! Christine! I need to talk to you. The shell man has gone, and I think he may have got my treasure." There was no answer.

The tramp started running like a mad man around the church trying to find Christine.

He didn't realise that he was running towards the cemetery. Suddenly he tripped over a grave stone that he didn't remember being there. It looked new.

The tramp was intrigued to know who had been buried-there wasn't anybody here bar the shop keepers, inn keeper, Christine and her husband whom he hadn't seen, and the shell man.

He looked at the inscription on the headstone. It read:

Here lies Captain Wirgoil
Died of the challenge 1969

"Oh no, not another one, so who's this then?" Then it suddenly dawned on him that it must be the shell man. The tramp was worried but happy at the same time. He knew that if the shell man was dead then he wouldn't be able to get his treasure.

"He's died of the challenge like all the others. What's going on here?" muttered the tramp.

"I'm not going to die of the challenge, I know that - they must have all done something wrong but I'm clever. This won't happen to me."

The tramp thought about the terms and conditions of the challenge. It stated that if you were unable to pay all your food bills in full by the end of June you wouldn't be allowed to get any food and drink so you would starve or die of thirst. The tramp had already found out that it wasn't possible to store any food or drink, because any food that you had left over wouldn't be edible the next day.

He had no idea what was going wrong - he was well up to the target of collecting enough shells to be able to fulfil the challenge, so there was no problem there.

Chapter Five: Completing The Challenge

The tramp carried on collecting the shells and in March 1970 he finally reached the target of the 10 sacks of 1000 shells - he had been very careful to make sure everyone was perfect but he didn't need to worry because if a shell wasn't perfect it was mysteriously thrown out of the sack. He had counted 10,056 shells so he had fifty six shells spare - he didn't want anything to go wrong.

As he expected the challenge had been very easy and had been fun [money for old rope] was the expression that he frequently used. It was time for him to find Christine. He didn't know what he had to do to get the treasure, and had no idea as to where it was. Only Christine knew that, so he had to find her. He knew that she wasn't at the church, and he hadn't seen her anywhere in the village. The only place that he thought that she could be was at Darridy, House the big house on the cliff.

The tramp was very excited. He knew that he would soon be a very wealthy man, and would get out of this place, which wouldn't be a day too soon for him. It had always been his dream to be a rich man, and he knew that it wouldn't be long now - his mind was on those ten caskets of treasure that he'd seen several months ago, they were now his. Nobody could deny that. He had got the 10 sacks of 1000 shells and every one was perfect. He had fulfilled everything the challenge terms had stated. And now he wanted his treasure.

The tramp started to walk up the steep steps to the big house. He could smell something really horrible as he was walking. It didn't take him long to realise that the smell was him!! He hadn't washed since he came into this place. He'd criticized the shell man but he was now the same - his hair and beard were long and he stank to high heaven. He made his way up the steps. He didn't run out of breath now, he was very fit. Collecting the shells had made him healthy.

He finally reached the house - everything was exactly as he remembered it. He went inside. It sent shivers down his spine being in this place but he carried on. He went up the stairs to the bedroom that he had found to be untouched when he was last here. The door was locked. He knocked on it, and shouted out, "Christine! Are you in there?"

The door slowly opened - the tramp stepped back, he was a little bit scared.

Christine was standing there. She seemed to be adjusting her head! Like she was putting it on!! She was jerking violently. "Hello Captain, I was expecting you to call me today. You've got the ten sacks of shells haven't you?"

"Yeah, I have," said the tramp proudly. The tramp couldn't help noticing that she was wearing the same clothes as she was wearing when he first met her.

"How have you been ma'am? I haven't seen you for a long time."

Christine didn't answer the question. "I suppose you want to know how to get the treasure."

"Well yes ma'am, that's why I've come looking for you - I'm sorry about the stink!! But I can't wash here. Um, you said, and as you know I have it in writing, that when I'd fulfilled the challenge

I would get the treasure, and you did say, all the treasure, ma'am. So I've come here to claim my reward. It is rightfully mine now, isn't it?"

"Yes, that's right - the person who fulfils the challenge will get the treasure. Are you sure you have followed all the terms of the challenge, because it's very important?"

"Yes, ma'am, I've been very careful - I've got the required ten sacks of one thousand shells and to make sure, I've got fifty six shells spare. I know that all the shells are perfect, because they get thrown out of the sacks if they are not."

"Then the treasure will be yours," Christine spoke softly and eloquently.

"Ah, that's brilliant. I'm so pleased that I accepted the challenge. It was a no – brainer, really, ma'am. I mean, I knew before I signed the contract that I would easily be able to do it. I'm quite intelligent. Ma'am how do I get my treasure?" The tramp was very excited now.

"You have to do something first - it's only a formality but it's part of the terms of being able to claim it."

"But why wasn't I told about this before I signed the contract?" The tramp seemed annoyed.

"Don't worry, it's nothing really. It's just a ritual to make sure that you're the person who has fulfilled the challenge. You have nothing to worry about."

Christine picked up the book that was on the bedroom side table. The same book that the tramp had tried to pick up when he came into this room. She opened it up on to a certain page.

"Captain you have to take the ten sacks down to the sea and place them at the water's edge and recite this verse:

> *"Captain Wirgoil here I be*
> *With the ten sacks by the sea*
>
> *I'm sorry that I stole your treasure*
> *None of it was for my pleasure*
>
> *As you know it was never spent*

You told me that it was for the heaven sent

Your challenge couldn't have been worse
Please release me from your curse

Take these ten sacks owed to thee
And let us all set out to sea."

"So I have to take the ten sacks down to the sea and place them at the water's edge and recite that verse, and then the treasure will be mine."

"That's right, Captain," said Christine placing the book back down on the table.

"Ah, well that sounds simple enough. It all seems silly to me though, but if that's how it has to be, well so be it."

"There's one thing, Captain, that's very important - you have to recite the verse exactly as written, if you don't, you won't get your treasure. Would you like me to recite it one more time for you?"

"No ma'am that won't be necessary. I can remember it word for word. It's all rhyming. It's easy to remember.

Well thank you for everything, ma'am. I probably won't see you again - can you say goodbye to the baker, butcher, grocer, and of course the inn keeper? So I'll say goodbye and hope that everything works out for you. I'm off to the South of France to buy a Chateau as soon as I get out of here. I'm going to buy a big expensive car as well. I really believe that I've earned it.

Well, goodbye. And thank you for making me rich."

The tramp walked back down the cliff steps reciting the verse, so that he would remember it

At this moment in time he felt the happiest man in the world. He knew that within the hour he would become a millionaire.

He walked onto the beach. As he walked, he was singing out loud, he was so happy.

He had one last job to do - to move the sacks down to the sea front. He carefully lined up the ten sacks into a neat line. He counted them to make sure that there were ten sacks. Everything was now ready.

He coughed and cleared his throat - he went through the verse in his mind to make sure that he knew it off by heart. He was confident that he did, so he began:

> *"Captain Wirgoil here I be*
> *With the ten sacks by the sea*
>
> *I'm sorry that I stole your treasure*
> *None of it was for my pleasure*
>
> *As you know it was never spent*
> *You told me that it was for the heaven sent*
>
> *Your challenge couldn't have been worse*
> *Please release me from your curse.*
>
> *Take these ten sacks owed to thee*
> *And let us all set out to sea."*

There that's done, isn't this exciting? I wonder what's going to happen?"

The tramp stood there for fifteen minutes, and nothing happened but he didn't know what was supposed to happen, as far as he was concerned he had fulfilled the challenge. He had ten sacks of one thousand shells lined up at the water's edge, and had recited the verse.

Twenty five minutes passed, still nothing, so he recited the verse again. But nothing happened.

He started losing his temper. "Where's my treasure?" he shouted out. "Come on, I was promised. I've done the challenge, now I want the treasure, come on give it to me."

Nothing was happening - suddenly the church clock chimed twelve times. It was opening time for the shops.

The tramp stormed off towards the shops, he thought that he'd ask the baker what was going on and why hadn't he got his treasure. He went into the baker's in a foul mood. "Where's my treasure?" he shouted to the baker.

"I've got the sacks of shells all lined up- I've been collecting for months, and it's been really hard work -where's the treasure, baker?"

"Hello, Captain - here's your food. Will there be anything else?"

"Yeah, ten caskets of treasure, where is it?" shouted the tramp.

"Can't do that, Captain. Is there anything else?"

"Oh, give me a hot Cornish pasty will you?" the tramp was very grumpy.

"Certainly, Captain. That'll be **512** pieces of gold, please, aye, **512** pieces of gold."

"What? Oh, no, it's the end of the blinking month!!I've got to pay the bills. I forgot about that - I'll have to take some shells out of the sacks."

The tramp went back to the beach and took out 2048 shells to pay for his monthly bill.

This left him with only **8008 shells.** He was short. He couldn't make the ten sacks of one thousand shells.

He now remembered what the challenge had said. You had to pay your food and drink bills on the last day of the month -but by paying them he wouldn't be able to have enough shells to **ever** complete the challenge.

The challenge had been set-up so that you could collect the ten sacks of one thousand shells on the very last day of March. But the amount of the bills were doubling- next month's bill would be 4096 shells and in May the bills would be a staggering 8192 shells. He would end up at the end of May minus 1860 shells and the challenge starts again in June. He'll only be able to collect 1210 shells. He wouldn't be able to pay off his bills in full.

The tramp wasn't able to pay off his bill to the grocer. He only had 188 shells left after paying the inn keeper, the baker, and butcher. The grocer wouldn't give the tramp any provisions, because he never had enough shells to pay off his bill in full. The grocer told him to hand over the shells that he had left otherwise he wouldn't be able to leave the shop. The tramp reluctantly handed over his last remaining shells but he already knew that this was likely to happen. He knew that this was nearly the end for him.

The challenge stated that he had to pay all his bills in full by the end of June but he would be **654** shells short, so he wouldn't be able to get any food and drink. He would have failed the challenge and die the following month. He now knew why there were so many Captain Wirgoils in the cemetery, and why they had all died of the challenge. They had all died of hunger and thirst. He now realised that whoever accepted the challenge, became Captain Wirgoil.

The tramp was allowed to start the challenge again on the first day of June but he wouldn't be allowed to get any provisions from the grocer who he owed the 1860 shells to. The tramp had a bit of a problem. He had chosen to pay off the butcher, baker and the inn keeper but the grocer supplied the drinking water. The tramp for a whole month had to survive drinking ale.

All that it did to accept the challenge was to prolong your life for the time you were in the village, because if you didn't accept the challenge, you would die sooner.

Nobody ever leaves this place. Greed was the lure for the tramp; greed was the reason for the loss of all the poor souls that had ever been to this place. While those ten caskets of treasure were here. It would never change. The challenge appeared to be easy but in reality it was impossible.

The tramp realised that he was now one of the lost souls.

Chapter Six: The New Man

It's the last day of May 1970. A young man aged 22 is walking along a hillside road somewhere in Cornwall. England. It's 10:30 am and it's a beautiful sunny morning, there's not a cloud in the sky.

This young man unlike all the others who have found themselves here on this day on this road at this time, hadn't done anything wrong. All his life, he'd felt that he was a lost soul. Things got much worse for him though, he's dying, he's only been given one year to live. He's found himself here today by something that happened to him several months ago.

It was the exact day that he was told that he had a terminal illness.

An old woman had come up to him and placed something in his hand and said, "This belongs to you. Fulfil what's asked of you, and all will be as it should be."

The young man had no idea as to what she was talking about. He looked at what she had placed into his hand - it was a gold coin dated 1665. It came from a country that he had never heard of.

The gold coin was the catalyst that had guided him here today - like the tramp who was guided by the old pram - the coin was the guider for this man.

As he walks along the top of the hillside road, he can see a village - something is different from last year and all other years. Nobody had ever been able to see the village until they were inside it. The young man [his name is Robert] likes the look of the village and quite fancies going to it, but he can't see any way in. Robert sits under a tree to get out of the sun. He's feeling very tired, his illness is taking effect. He falls fast asleep, and as he sleeps, a thick mist had got up and passed over him.

A short while later he woke up, and to his surprise a path had mysteriously appeared which seemed to lead down to the village. Robert made his way onto the path. He didn't have to be forced, he wanted to go down it. As he walked down, it got steeper and steeper, until he found himself having to run. When he reached the end of the path, there was no gate.

The path went straight into the village. Robert didn't see any bones or skulls and the grass was fresh and green - there were trees and beautiful flowers in abundance. Birds and butterflies were everywhere. This place was what Robert thought the garden of Eden must have been like. It was idyllic - just what he was looking for to spend his last days on Earth.

Robert had been a caring person but when he became ill, he just wanted to be alone. He decided that he would explore the beautiful countryside of England. He never complained, he had accepted his fate with dignity.

He saw the church to his left and decided to explore it - he loved churches but he wasn't a religious person,. He didn't really know if there was a God. He opened the two large arched oak doors and walked inside. He found this to be a beautiful, tranquil place. He sat down on a pew and said a little prayer - just in case there was somebody special that may be listening to him. This made him feel better.

He got up from the pew, and like the tramp he made his way to the cemetery, but unlike the tramp and everyone else that had been here, he didn't see any descriptions of anybody called Captain Wirgoil. All the grave stones were normal names of people and dates that dated back to the 17th century.

Robert walked away from the church and came upon a sign which he assumed was the name of the village, it read:

FRIENDSHIP COVE

He could see the church clock from where he was standing - it read that it was 11am.

He looked at his watch, the clock was spot on. He walked further along and came to the village green and the bench. He sat down. He could see the three shops and the inn but they were all closed. He closed his eyes and meditated, he felt at peace here.

An hour quickly went by, he was taken out of his meditation by the chimes of the church clock.

It was 12 pm. The shops opened their doors for business but Robert hadn't seen anybody in this village and wondered where the people were. Just like the tramp before him, the smell of the bread coming from the baker's was enticing him. He really fancied a loaf of fresh bread but he didn't have any money.

Suddenly his nose picked up a horrendous smell that completely masked out the smell from the bread. Coming down the path he caught sight of the dirtiest person that he had ever seen. "What a sight!", thought Robert. But he'd had troubles himself - so he thought who was he to judge this man, nobody could know what has led him to be the way that he finds himself today.

A tramp came walking along. He had a lost forlorn look on his face. It was obvious to Robert that this man had the troubles of the world on his shoulders. The tramp had to pass Robert. "Hello." said Robert "It's a nice day isn't it?"

But the tramp didn't say anything.

"You're the first person that I've seen in this village, where are all the other people?"

Once again the tramp ignored him.

"Sir, I don't suppose you could spare a bit of small change so that I can get a loaf of bread, can you? I don't have any money."

"Too bad," said the tramp arrogantly, "you'll not get a penny from me. What are you doing in this horrible place? I suppose you've been lured here." The tramp grinned.

"No, I haven't been "lured" here. I wanted to come. I saw the village from the top of the hill and I liked it - it's beautiful!"

The tramp laughed. "Beautiful!" Are you crazy? There's nothing beautiful about this place - it's a hell hole."

"No it's not! - it's beautiful here and the air is fresh and sweet and the flowers and birds and butterflies are wonderful. I'm going to stay here for a while."

"You'll be staying a lot longer than that," said the tramp. "You can't get out of this place. You're a prisoner now."

"No, I'm not, I can go anytime I want," said Robert. As he spoke a butterfly flew down and settled on his arm. "Look at that, isn't that beautiful?"

"What's beautiful?"

"This butterfly that's on my arm," said Robert passionately.

"There's nothing there, mate - you're going off your rocker. There's no life here at all, except for the three shopkeepers and Christine, and I'm not sure if they're alive?. I don't know what they are. Look like zombies to me. There used to be another dirty old man who I called the shell man but he's gone now. I'm glad of that, because he stank! I'll tell you one thing, mate. The ...." suddenly the tramp couldn't get the words out of his mouth. It was like he was being gagged. He wanted to say, "... challenge is impossible."

The tramp walked off and went into the baker's. Robert followed him in.

The baker handed the tramp his bag of food and asked him if there was anything else.

"No!" shouted the tramp angrily.

"Fine captain, that'll be 2048 pieces of gold. Aye, 2048 pieces of gold."

The tramp handed the baker a big bag of sea shells. The tramp knew that this would be the last time that he would be able pay the baker with shells. The baker emptied the bag of shells on the counter and counted them. He seemed to be able to count them very quickly.

"That'll be fine Captain, aye, fine."

"Hang on a minute," said Robert. "Did I just hear the baker ask you for 2048 pieces of gold and you gave him a bag of shells? What's all that about?"

"You'll soon find out," said the tramp. "Don't accept the ..." he wanted to say "challenge" but couldn't get the words out of his mouth.

"Hello, baker." Robert didn't see the baker as a pirate. He saw him as a normal man, and he wasn't wearing a mask.

"Hello, Robert," said the baker politely.

"How do you know my name?"

"We've been waiting for you. Have been for a long time. It's good to see you at last.

Now then, what can I get for you?"

"I don't have any money to be able to buy anything. Is it possible for me to earn a loaf of bread by doing some work for you?"

"That won't be necessary - you have a coin. Can I see it?"

"How did you know about the coin?" Robert was thinking that this was all getting very strange.

He took the gold coin out of his pocket and was about to hand it to the baker.

"No, no, I'm not allowed to touch it - that will be fine sir. Here's your bread, would you like anything else?"

"No. I'm happy with that. It's most kind of you to give me the bread, thank you."

Robert went out of the baker's and sat on the village green bench and ate the bread.

When he had finished the bread, he was very thirsty and fancied a pint of beer so he went to the inn. Inside the inn was the tramp sitting at a table, and he appeared to be talking to himself.

"Hello, again," said Robert to the tramp. "That's just what I fancy, a nice pint of beer. Can't remember the last time I had a pint."

The tramp didn't say anything, he was just muttering away to himself.

"Barman, I haven't got any money, and I really fancy a pint of beer - is it possible to do some work for you for a beer?"

"That won't be necessary, Robert - you've got a coin. Can I see it please?"

Robert showed the barman the coin. The barman looked like a normal person to Robert but he was dressed in 17th century clothing as was the baker.

Robert was really puzzled how they all seemed to know his name and that he had the coin.

"That will be fine sir, here's your ale, enjoy." The barman handed Robert his ale in a metal tankard.

"How do you know my name, and how do you know that I've got the coin?"

"Because I do, and that's all there is to it," said the barman rather nonchalantly.

"Well it can't be 'all there is to it,' as you call it. What's going on here?"

The barman didn't answer.

Robert sat down at the next table to the tramp. "Do you know what's going on in this village? I'm sorry I don't know your name but I heard the baker call you "Captain". Is that what you are? What ship are you captaining?"

The tramp laughed, "No, I'm not a captain, and you don't want to be one either, if you know what's good for you. And yeah, I do know what's going here but I wouldn't be allowed to tell you, so don't bother to ask."

"Can you just tell me one thing, how come you pay for your stuff with sea shells?"

"Because I accepted the…" The tramp couldn't get the word "challenge" out of his mouth.

"I told you, I'm not allowed to tell you anything. You have to find out for yourself. Ask Christine."

"Most odd," thought Robert.

When Robert finished his beer he went outside for a breath of fresh air.

It wasn't long before the tramp came out of the inn - he was holding two bags - one large and one small bag of shells on his back. He walked into the butcher's. Robert followed him, just to see what was going on. The tramp was greeted by the butcher with the same statement as the baker had made. The tramp handed over one sack of shells, the larger one. The butcher counted them. He seemed to be able to count them very quickly.

"Aye that'll be fine, Captain, fine," the butcher spoke in a pirate voice but when it came to Robert he spoke in a different accent, just like the baker and the barman.

"What can I do for you, Robert?" asked the butcher.

"Nothing, I don't want anything - but can you tell me what's going on here?"

"What do you mean?" asked the butcher, looking puzzled.

"Well you seem to know my name, and you talk to that man in a pirate accent but when you talk to me it's completely different. Why?"

"I don't know what you mean. I always talk, as I talk", said the butcher.

"No you don't, neither does the baker, or the inn keeper, and you call this man "Captain" and he says that he isn't a Captain, and why are you letting him pay you with sea shells?"

"They're not sea shells, Robert – they're gold pieces."

"What? No! Are you crazy? It's clear as daylight that they're sea shells, how could you possibly think that they're gold?"

Robert took his gold coin out of his pocket. "This is gold!" And he picked up one of the tramp's sea shells. "This is a sea shell! can't you see the difference?"

The butcher shook his head, as a gesture to express that he didn't.

The tramp went into the grocer's but Robert didn't follow him in this time - he didn't need anything from the grocer. A few minutes later the tramp came out mumbling to himself. He looked so miserable. All of his bags were now gone but the tramp didn't seem to have got anything from the grocer. The tramp made his way back to the beach. Robert went and sat on the village green bench. About ten minutes later the church clock chimed one, and all the shops, and the inn closed.

Chapter Seven: Robert Meets Christine

As Robert was sitting there reflecting on what was happening here, he caught sight of a rather beautiful woman dressed in 17th century clothing coming towards him. Just like the shopkeepers and the inn keeper. Christine looked like a normal person to Robert.

"Hello ma'am, it's a fine day, isn't it? And it's certainly a beautiful village that you have here. I'm a stranger, but I'm a bit baffled as to what's going on here in this village. Who is that tramp? And why does he pay for his bills with sea shells? And everybody seems to know who I am but I've never been here before. I would like to stay. I don't have any money though, so I would need to find paid work of some kind. I don't mind what I do as long as it's not too hard, because I'm not very well."

"Hello, Robert, my name is Christine. I can answer some of your questions. The reason why that man pays his bills with sea shells, is because he accepted a challenge. So if you want to stay here and be able to buy your food with sea shells you'll have to accept the challenge. But be warned you will have to stay here until you have fulfilled it, you won't be able to leave."

"That sounds interesting - so I don't need any money then? And collecting shells is not hard work, I can do that."

Robert seemed happy that he could stay here and be fed by paying for his food with sea shells - it seemed to him too good to be true.

"What's the challenge ma'am?"

Christine explained the rules of the challenge to Robert. He sat there thinking about it - he was very good at mathematics. Robert knelt down on the damp sand and smoothed it out with the back of his hand to make it like a blackboard. He started to scribe numbers with his finger in the sand. He knew that it could be a conundrum but he wasn't sure. There was something in his mind that he'd heard a long time ago that had stuck in his memory.

A person was asked to put grains of rice on a chess board, doubling upon each square. The lesson was that there wouldn't be enough rice in China to be able to cover all the squares of the chess board. Which surprised Robert when he heard it.

The challenge was something similar to this - it seemed easy but Robert felt that there might be a catch somewhere. He had to try and work out where the catch was. He knelt there for quite a long time. His fingers were working the maths of the equation out in the damp sand. The figures were getting longer, and longer. After about ten minutes Robert was able to make a calculation.

"Christine..." Robert paused for a moment, "...I think the challenge is impossible ma'am, although it sounds easy. I think that it's a conundrum. I've heard of something like this before. Anybody who accepts this challenge would die of hunger and thirst in the month of July of the following year."

Robert was spot on. He'd worked out the maths of it extremely well.

"I think I know of a way that it would be possible for it to be achieved though, Christine."

Christine was just standing there motionless. It was like she was expecting him to work it out. She smiled.

Robert suddenly remembered the words of the old woman who had given him the gold coin,

"...fulfil what is asked of you, and all will be as it should be."

He didn't know what it meant at the time but he knew that this is what she must have been talking about. But he had no idea what "... all will be as it should be" meant.

"Christine, I will accept the challenge. Is that what that poor tramp is doing? Did he accept the challenge?"

"Yes he did. They all did," Christine paused. Robert could tell that she was troubled.

"A lot of people have tried and they have all failed, and now they're all dead, and I'm really sorry. We think, though, that you will be the one who will be able to fulfil it. There's great treasure for the person who achieves it - would you like to see it?"

"No, thanks ma'am - treasure is of no use to me."

There were thoughts in Robert's mind that he didn't understand.

"Christine you say that I can buy my food and drink with sea shells but the shopkeepers and inn keeper allow me to get my food already, because I have a coin. Why should I collect shells when I can have the food for nothing?"

"Good question Robert, There is an answer. If you don't want the treasure then you're allowed a wish - if you fulfil the challenge then your wish will come true but you must not wish for wealth. Once you accept the challenge, you'll no longer be able to use the coin. It's your choice, you're free to leave if you want to."

Robert fully understood the consequences of her answer, and he knew that he had nothing to lose, so he signed the challenge document and made his wish. He didn't expect it to come to anything; he knew that wishes rarely come true. Christine nodded her head. She seemed to know what Robert had wished for.

Robert made his way to the beach to start collecting sea shells but the tide was in. He couldn't collect any shells, so he decided to go for a walk along the beach. The rock formation was blocking the view out to sea. The sunken ship was still there but he couldn't see it, because the tide was in, so some things were the same as the tramp could see.

It was a very hot day, as it always is here. Robert decided to go for a swim. He took off his clothes to his underpants. He was just about to dive into the water, when he heard the tramp screaming at him.

"No, don't do that, the water is freezing!"

"Is it?" Robert put his hand into the water, it felt warm. "No, it's warm, why don't you go in and clean yourself? It would make you feel better," he told the tramp.

"I not going in there- I'll die instantly," said the tramp shaking his head in disapproval of such a ridiculous suggestion.

"Die of what? Being clean?" Robert laughed.

"No, the cold water! It's freezing! Nobody would last long in that water. You're trying to kill me, aren't you? I know you're game."

"Don't be silly," said Robert, "I'm just trying to get you to wash. It's not cold! I'll show you."

Robert dived into the water and started swimming around.

"It's great in here, and it certainly isn't cold. Come on, come in, it will do you good."

The tramp walked to the water's edge. He hadn't tested it since the day that he was first in here. He put his foot into the water and yelled out, like he was in some sort of great pain.

"It's freezing! I can't go in. I don't know how you're able to stay in there," moaned the tramp banging his foot up and down on the ground trying to get the blood to circulate back into it.

After a few minutes Robert came out. He felt very refreshed.

"I suppose you're waiting for the tide to go out so you can start collecting those shells?" said Robert to the tramp.

"What's it got to do with you?" said the tramp abruptly.

"Well, I'm going to be collecting as well. I'm not after the treasure though - I'm collecting just to buy food with the shells. You know the challenge is impossible, don't you?"

"Well I do now," said the tramp. "But I didn't, before I signed the contract. If you know that it's impossible, why did you accept the challenge?"

"Because I like it here, and it seems a good deal to me just to collect sea shells for food and drink for a year, because that's all the time that anybody would have here. You know that you won't be able to buy any more food and drink from the first of July, don't you?"

The tramp looked down at the sand and with a sad voice said that he did.

"Oh, dear you are in a pickle, aren't you? No food - and no treasure for you then?"

The tramp sighed. He knew his fate. He had done so for several months.

"Now let me see, how many shells are you going to be short of, at the end of this month? That'll be 1860." Robert already knew the answer," You couldn't pay off one of your bills, could you?"

The tramp nodded his head to indicate that Robert was correct,

"Um, at the end of the next month, June you'll have to pay 1864. That leaves you 654 shells short. The terms stated that you had to pay off all your bills at the end of June. So you're not going to make it, are you, mate?"

Robert was playing games with the tramp but he knew of a way to help him.

Chapter Eight: The Challenge is Fulfilled

"**N**ow let me think, um, I'll be able to collect 1210 shells, and I've got to pay four shells tomorrow for my food and drink, so at the end of the month I'll have 1206 left - that's plenty, isn't it?"

"Plenty for you but not for *me*," moaned the tramp.

"Well, the solution is a simple one. Do you want to stay alive?"

"Of course I do, but how can I? It's impossible. I've failed already."

The tramp looked glum.

"No it's not impossible," said Robert with a smile on his face. "All that I have to do is give you 654 of my shells at the end of the month. You'll be able to pay off your bills in full, and you'll be able to continue the challenge. How's that sound?"

"Why would you do that?" said the tramp not believing what he was hearing,

"Why? Because, it doesn't matter to me, I've only got a year of my life left anyway, I've got a terminal illness. That's why."

"Oh, I'm sorry to hear that" said the tramp trying to show some sympathy but his true feelings were the opposite. "Well, thank you, what more can I say?"

"Nothing," said Robert "Nothing at all, I'm happy to help you."

The tramp was so cheered up now that he did a little dance on the sand. But there was more good news to come for him.

Robert had worked out how it would be possible to fulfil the challenge. If he gave the tramp his shells when they had both collected enough, the tramp would be able to have the ten sacks of one thousand shells and would have paid all his bills in full.

The challenge would be completed and the tramp would have the treasure. It didn't matter to Robert as he wasn't going to survive anyway. He was going to lose his life but at least this way he was saving a life.

He told the tramp of his plan. The tramp went hysterical; one minute he was preparing himself to die, and now he was not only going to live but he would also fulfil his dreams of becoming a very wealthy man.

He got hold of Robert and hugged and kissed him.

"How did you work it out when everyone else had failed?" asked the tramp.

"Because the challenge is based on greed, sir - there are always for a short period of time, two people in this place doing the challenge. If they helped each other, or should I say, in my case, if I helped you - like I'm going to... then it's not an impossibility anymore - it's certain that the one who gets the help will fulfil the challenge.

*

As promised Robert paid what the tramp owed, and they both carried on collecting the shells. There was harmony on the beach which Robert was glad of, although the tramp wasn't very good company, and he stank!

In November Robert had collected 6354 shells and had paid off his food and drink bills. The tramp had 5802 shells after paying his bills - so they were now in a position to be able to fulfil the challenge.

THE CHALLENGE CALCULATOR
The Tramp

Month	Shell's collected	Cost of food	Shell's left
JUNE	1210	4	1206
JULY	2416	8	2408
AUGUST	3618	16	3602
SEPTEMBER	4812	32	4780
OCTOBER	5990	64	5926
NOVEMBER	7136	128	7008
DECEMBER	8218	256	7962
JANUARY	9172	512	8660
FEBRUARY	9870	1024	8846
MARCH	10056	2048	8008
APRIL	9218	4096	5122
MAY	6332	8192	-1860

The tramp was unable to pay all his food bills off at the end of May - each shop and the inn wanted 2048 shells but he could only pay three of them. He would no longer be able to get any food or drink from one of the shops or the inn. The challenge would start again in June.

He would be able to get provisions from three of them.

THE NEW YEAR
THE CHALLENGE BEGINS AGAIN
The Tramp

JUNE	1210	4	-654

The tramp was not able to pay off all his bills in full. Under the terms of the challenge he would no longer be able to get any more food so would starve to death.

Robert the new man in the village had collected 1210 shells and gave the tramp 654 to pay off his bills. He would now be able to continue the challenge.

	ROBERT			THE TRAMP		
	Shells collected	Cost	Shell's left	Shells collected	Cost	Shells left
JUNE	1210	4	552	1210	4	0
JULY	1726	8	1754	1210	8	1202
AUGUST	2964	16	2948	2412	16	2396
SEPTEMBER	4158	32	4126	3606	32	3574
OCTOBER	5336	64	5272	4784	64	4720
NOVEMBER	6482	128	6354	5930	128	5802

At the end of November, Robert and the tramp had a combined total of 12156 shells. Robert gave the tramp 4198 shells to make up his total to 10,000. The tramp would now be able to fulfil the challenge.

Robert's health had deteriorated. He felt very unwell now. He knew that he only had a few months to live. But he was happy that he was now able to help the tramp. Everything was now ready. Robert helped the tramp to carry the sacks of shells down to the beach and place them in the water as requested by the challenge document.

Robert didn't know what was to happen next. He asked the tramp but the tramp was not willing to tell him. He had suddenly turned into a *fiend*; the thought of the treasure was making him turn like all the other people that had ever seen the treasure. Ruthless! Greedy!

He told Robert to go away, and said that he didn't trust him, and that he'd not be getting any of *his* treasure, and he made it known to him that all the treasure was to go to the person who fulfils the challenge, and that was *him*.

Robert walked back up the beach and sat down on the sand to watch.

He could see the tramp moving his arms about, and could hear him reciting a verse.

The tramp stood there with his hands outstretched to the sea, like he was beckoning someone to come to him. A few moments later, something started to happen. A thick mist, more of a cloud got up from the sea and was coming toward the tramp.

Suddenly the baker, butcher, grocer and inn keeper walked past Robert and headed toward the tramp.

"What are you doing here?" shouted the tramp. "You're not getting any of *my* treasure. Go away! It's *mine*, all *mine*. I've fulfilled the challenge." He was like a man possessed.

"None of you thought that I could do it but *I'm* so clever, I've outwitted you all."

Then the tramp could see Christine coming towards him.

"Christine!" shouted the tramp excitedly. "I've fulfilled the challenge, and I've spoken that stupid verse. Where's *my* treasure? Take me to it now. I demand you to take me to what is rightfully mine - I want to get out of this place. I worked it out all by myself of how to fulfil the challenge. I fooled that stupid new man into helping me, he gave me some of his shells.

I told you that I was clever, didn't I? What a fool he is! But he's dying anyway so he won't need any money where he's going. Now then, I want my treasure - where is it?" The tramp was raving and ranting and was telling a load of lies. He didn't deserve to have the treasure.

"Soon, Captain - You are Captain Wirgoil, aren't you? It's important that you are, because you'll have your reward soon," said Christine in a soft voice.

"Well, of course, I'm Captain Wirgoil," said the tramp confidently.

"Well that's fine then, Captain. It's definitely your treasure."

"Good," said the tramp, "I'm glad that we've sorted that out. So where is it?"

The butcher, baker, grocer and the inn keeper all shouted out at the same time,

"Aye., Aye Captain, it won't be long now sir." It was like they were all very happy.

Christine waved to Robert - he waved back to her but he felt that she was waving 'goodbye'.

Suddenly the dark cloud was over them: then something strange happened.

It started raining and it was heavy. It never rained in this place. Lightning streaked across the dark sky, and there was a roar of thunder. It felt like somebody was angry up in the heavens.

The tramp stood there dumbfounded.

"What's happening? It never rains here," he yelled.

The heavy rain was washing the dirt from his face. Streaks of light and dark were marking his face where it was possible to see skin.

The dark cloud passed, and it was sunny again.

"What was that all about?" the tramp asked Christine but she didn't answer.

Something strange had happened during the storm. The sunken ship had risen from the sea bed.

The tramp was petrified. He sensed that there was something behind him. He turned around expecting to see the three shop keepers, the inn keeper and Christine.

But he wasn't prepared for what was there. He screamed! It was the scream of a person who felt that their life was immediately about to end.

Behind him were five skeletal people. The butcher, baker, grocer, the inn keeper and Christine had all shed their clothes and masks but they were still wearing their wigs.

Robert was witnessing what was taking place and was horrified, but there was nothing that he could do.

The tramp fell to his knees and shouted "What have I done? What have I done?"

The ship sent out a large rowing boat. Aboard the boat were six skeleton rowers and a skeleton who was wearing a Captain's hat; he was standing at the front of the rowing boat and was directing things. The rowing boat came in to the shore.

"Hello, Christine," said the skeleton wearing the Captain's hat.

"Hello, Mr Bradshaw," replied Christine waving her skeletal hand to him.

"Hello, Captain Wirgoil. It's been a long time, sir," said Mr Bradshaw, "I see that you've brought our treasure at last." Mr. Bradshaw was pointing at the tramp.

"No! -No! You've made a mistake, I'm not Captain Wirgoil. I'm a tramp, and I've been doing a challenge, which I've completed. And this is not treasure, they're only sea shells. Just ten sacks of useless sea shells. They're not worth anything at all."

The tramp was hysterical. He was frightened at what was happening here.

"It's gold, Captain. Isn't that right, Christine?" said Mr. Bradshaw who spoke with a posh English accent.

Christine nodded her head, which made her head wobble. She had to use her skeletal hand to steady it. Her wig was skewed which she adjusted. She had always liked to look her best when she was alive.

"No! It's not gold," shouted the tramp, "here, I'll show you."

The tramp took a handful of the shells out of one of the sacks and showed Mr Bradshaw the shells.

"Yes, that's it, that's our gold, Captain, bring it aboard, sir and we'll all be on our way. We'll all be rich now."

"No!" shouted the tramp you won't be rich - they're sea shells, they're not worth anything, but there is gold here, and it's all mine. I fulfilled the challenge, and I won it. I'll share it with you."

The tramp paused, he was thinking about the situation that he found himself in.

"No. I'll tell you what? You can have it all. I just want to get out of this horrible place. I don't want to be rich anymore."

"But, Captain, you didn't fulfill the challenge," Said Mr. Bradshaw, motioning his skeletal hand for the tramp to come aboard.

"How many times do I have to tell you? I'm not Captain Wirgoil. I'm a tramp!"

"You're Captain Wirgoil," said Mr Bradshaw, "and we accept your apology. Now, come on, we've got to set sail. And bring our gold, Captain."

"But it's not gold!" shouted the tramp. "They're sea shells, how many more times do I have to tell you? Sea shells - sea-shells - sea-shells, that's all they are."

"It's gold, Captain, that's what you told us," said Mr Bradshaw. "So as far as we're concerned, if it's gold to you, then it's gold for us, isn't that right, Christine?"

"Yes." She paused. It was as if she didn't want to say the next few words.

"That's right, Mr Bradshaw. That's what we told you it was."

"Come on, now, Captain," said Christine grabbing hold of the tramp's hand, "it's time to go home. We've all been here too long – let's end it now. We've got to go back on our ship."

"No! I'm not going." shouted the tramp. "You can't make me. You're all dead people! How can this be? You promised me the treasure. I knew that there was something funny about you. Now let me go. I'm not going on that ship. I fulfilled the challenge you told me about, and I have a signed a contract that the treasure would be mine if I fulfilled the challenge. Which I did."

"No, Captain, Mr Bradshaw is correct. The treasure is for the one who fulfilled the challenge - you didn't fulfil the challenge,

Robert did. He fulfilled the challenge by giving you his shells, without his help, you wouldn't have been able to do it."

"Well take him aboard with you, and let me go," pleaded the tramp.

"Can't do that," said Christine, "whoever stands on the beach with the ten sacks of shells and recites the verse will become Captain Wirgoil and will get Captain Wirgoil's treasure which are the sea shells. And you confirmed to me that you were Captain Wirgoil, so the treasure is yours. Come on, Captain, we've got to go on the ship."

"Where we going?" asked the tramp in a trembling voice.

"We're going to Davy Jones' Locker, Captain," said Christine calmly.

"No!" screamed the tramp, "I'm not going there."

At those defiant words the butcher, baker, grocer and the inn keeper got hold of the tramp and manhandled him onto the rowing boat.

They put the ten sacks of sea shells on board as well. Mr Bradshaw helped Christine aboard the rowing boat, and they rowed to the ship.

Robert was watching everything that was happening, and was horrified. He thought that he was helping the tramp but it turned out to be something that he didn't expect. He saw for the first time that the three shop keepers, the inn keeper and Christine were, in reality, all dead people. He couldn't understand why he saw these people as they once were. And he didn't know why he wasn't called "Captain" like all the other people who had accepted the challenge. He watched the ship sail out of the cove, and wondered what fate the tramp would suffer. A few moments later the ship completely disappeared.

Chapter Nine: Finding The Treasure

As Robert was sitting there another thick sea mist suddenly sprung up - it quickly engulfed the entire village. After a few minutes the mist was gone, but the village was gone as well. There wasn't a sign that he could see of this village ever having been here. Even the rock formation out at sea had mysteriously disappeared - it was a clear sight out to sea now.

Robert suddenly realised that there was something different about him. He felt well. Just moments ago he had felt very ill, but now he felt fitter than he'd ever felt in his entire life.

He knew that there was no point in staying here. It was just a sandy cove now. He started to walk back to where the church had once stood. As he walked he stumbled on something that was sticking out of the ground. He picked it up. It was a book. He opened it up on the first page and could see that it was somebody's diary. He was shocked to see his name inscribed on the first page.

To Robert the heaven sent - your wish has been granted

Christine

Robert was puzzled by this statement but then he remembered what he had wished for. He'd wished to be well again and he did feel well. He wondered, could it be possible that his wish had come true? He really hoped so but he wouldn't know until he'd had tests done at the hospital.

Robert turned to the next page of the book. It was titled:

Captain Wirgoil's Diary
This book can only be read by the person who fulfils the challenge
It's the notes for the start

Robert could read it - he was surprised by that, because it stated that only the person who had fulfilled the challenge would be able to read it. He knew the tramp had fulfilled the challenge. He had no idea what "*it's the notes for the start*" meant. He thought that it must refer to the words of the diary. The diary gave an account of what had taken place. Robert started to read it. It read:

On the 16th of August 1668 The HMS CLEO-H set sail from Dover - it's mission was to locate a secret cove in Cornwall that was believed to be used by some notorious pirates to attack merchant ships. I, Captain Wirgoil, had myself been attacked in June 1666, off Cornwall, and left for dead - I saw three pirate ships come out from a formation of rocks. I felt that it was unusual for pirates to combine together to attack ships, but this is what they did and why they had been so successful. They had been terrorising this part of the coast for many years. Merchant ships were refusing to bring their cargoes to Britain.

I was sent out to escort a merchant ship past Cornwall. On board, that day, was the king of England's son and his newly-wed tribal wife, who were both killed.

The king's son put up a mighty fight but was overcome. I recognised three of the pirate leaders. One was a well-known person named "Rabbit Foot" He got his name because he always wore a rabbit foot around his neck for good luck. Another recognisable pirate was "Pretty Bob". He got his name because he wore a woman's dress when he attacked ships. This put people off from fighting him, because at first sight they thought that he was a woman. And then there was another rogue named "Skunk". Skunk stank so much that nobody would go near him.

All my men were killed - all the people on the merchant ship were killed - the ship's cargo was stolen. I was left for dead on my wreck of a ship. I only survived by drinking rain water. My ship drifted for eight days before being found. I had some terrible injuries, and was lucky to survive.

When I had recovered from my injuries, I, Captain Nigel Wirgoil, was asked by the king of England to find the rock formation and possible secret cove and kill all the pirates, as I was the only person who knew where it was.

I was newly- wed and was reluctant to leave my wife so I was given special permission by the king to take my wife, Christine, on the mission.

The ship had a crew of fifty men. My first mate was Mr. Bradshaw, and all the crew members had been specially chosen. The king was very angry that the pirates had killed his second son and wanted retribution.

We sailed to Cornwall to where I believed was a secret cove.

We waited for several days observing the rocks that I believe we were attacked from but nothing could be seen of the pirates. So I decided to take a crew of four men plus myself and row to the rocks and see if we could find a way in.

We eventually found the entrance. It was difficult to find, the pirates had chosen well.

The entrance led to a large cove that surprisingly had a village.

We found a horrendous carnage had taken place here - it appeared that the pirates had fought a battle to the death, to the very last man. I found the remains of "Skunk" and "Pretty Bob" and "Rabbit Foot" plus hundreds of other pirates.

We searched the cove and came across a cave. Inside the cave was the skeleton of a pirate that was lying across a metal casket. He had written in the sand a message. It read

"You can't eat gold
you can't drink gold
food and drink
is what I need
I would give everything
for a sip of water
and a piece of bread".

It appeared that this poor soul was the last pirate alive but he died of hunger and thirst.

I opened the casket and was shocked to see that it was filled to the brim with treasure. We found another nine caskets all filled with vast amounts of gold coins and beautiful jewellery.

It was obvious that this hoard was worth a king's ransom, and it explained why the pirates had fought a battle here - the pirates had got "treasure fever." We counted the gold coins - there were ten thousand in all. Unfortunately I, too, seeing so much wealth succumbed to the fever. So, too, my four- man crew.

We rowed back to our ship and informed the rest of the crew of our find. A vote was taken and it was decided that we would all share the treasure among ourselves. We had fulfilled our mission to find the cove and kill all the pirates, although they had killed themselves.

Nobody knew about the treasure, so we thought that we would keep it for ourselves,

We couldn't go back to Dover with such wealth, so it was decided that we would stay and live in the cove village for a few years and then disperse.

The cove was very secluded- it couldn't be seen from land or sea. There were the rocks that hid it from the sea, and huge sheer cliffs hid it from the land.

We sailed the CLEO-H into the cove and spent the next two years in the village. Every now and again we would do as the pirates had done and attack merchant ships for supplies.

In 1670 I informed the crew that myself and Christine and the four men who rowed in with us were going to stay at the village. I could see the signs of treasure fever festering amongst the crew members - all of them had seen the treasure, and mistrust was starting to manifest itself. They had all seen the aftermath of the battle that had been fought here by the pirates over the treasure. Nobody now trusted anyone. It was agreed that the crew would have the ten thousand gold coins and myself, Christine and the four crew members would have the jewellery. It was arranged that Mr. Bradshaw and six of the men would row in after getting the CLEO-H ready to sail and collect their treasure which would be put in ten sacks of one thousand gold coins per sack and left on the shore for them to collect.

Captain Nigel Wirgoil
Last day of May 1670

*

Robert finished reading Captain Wirgoil's diary. It didn't explain what happened next, but Robert could guess - it appeared that the Captain, Christine and the four crew members had set a trap for the crew of the CLEO-H and had put sea shells in the sacks instead of the treasure. A raging battle must then have taken place.

Captain Wirgoil and the four crew members fought a battle to death with the crew of the CLEO-H.

The CLEO-H had been sunk in the battle. The Captain and Christine and the four crew members were finally killed. A few of the CLEO-H crew members survived, but were unable to leave the cove. They eventually must have died of starvation and thirst.

87

At the back of the diary was a loose piece of paper that had been folded in between the pages. Robert looked at it and laughed. It appeared to be a treasure map. The map had been hand-written and drawn with instructions for where Captain Wirgoil's treasure was. The very last thing that he wanted at this moment in time was a treasure map. Robert threw the map away but it seemed to catch in a wind that sprung up from nowhere. It was a calm day, so Robert was puzzled where the wind had come from. Robert carried on walking. He was reflecting about Captain Wirgoil's diary. He couldn't help thinking that this whole sordid story was based upon greed.

Captain Wirgoil, all the men of the CLEO-H and all the pirates had all lost their lives for money.

Robert had no doubt that in time Captain Wirgoil was probably right. His men would have eventually turned on each other for the treasure. None of them would have been prepared to share, despite there being plenty for all the men.

As Robert walked up the path another strong gust of wind suddenly got up and the treasure map came fluttering down in front of his face. No matter where he walked, the map followed him. It seemed that Robert had no choice but to follow the map or the map would follow him wherever he went. He reluctantly plucked it from the air and started to scrutinise it.

The map showed the cove as it once was - it was exactly as Robert knew it before it disappeared. Where the church used to be there was an "X" that marked the first stone laid. Robert didn't know where this stone was because the church wasn't here anymore but the "X" marked the first steps that you had to follow. There was no stone here that he could see. The only clue that he had was the diary. There was something in Captain's Wirgoil's words that Robert felt didn't make any sense. He had written "It's the notes for the start." There wasn't any notes. Captain Wirgoil had written the account of the story in one go.

Robert thought that this could be a clue to the start of the treasure hunt. He read this line over and over again - he was sure that it was some kind of clue. The treasure map stated that he had to start at the first stone laid. Suddenly something clicked in his mind. The Captain had written the word "start" at the end of the sentence. Robert then saw what the Captain was telling him. It was the word "notes" It didn't refer to writing as Robert thought - it was the clue. If you rearrange the letters of the word notes, you could get the word stone! So the sentence was saying that… It's the stone for the start. The diary was the first stone laid. Robert hoped that's what it was saying but he didn't really know for sure.

He walked back to where the church would have been. He didn't really know what to do next. Suddenly the diary dropped out of his hand - he wasn't sure whether he had accidentally dropped it, or it had been forced from his hand. The diary fell to the ground and instantly turned to stone. An X appeared on it followed by an arrow. The map stated that you had to take eight steps forward. So Robert paced out the eight steps from the direction of the arrow. All the time he was laughing to himself. He knew that what he was doing was ridiculous. He'd seen plenty of pirate films, and there was always the predictable curse and, of course, a pirate map following treasure. All these things seem to go together. But he remembered that Christine had told him that there was treasure here. Robert thought that he had nothing to lose so he started following the treasure map.

The map told him to take ten steps to the left, so he did. Then, three steps to the right - Robert paced out the three steps. Four steps left was next - five steps left -six steps left - five steps right - six steps left - was the final instruction. The map had the letters "*T H*" with arrows pointing downwards. Robert wondered what the "*T H*" meant. He reasoned that it must mean (treasure here) but there was absolutely nothing here. He knew that he was standing on the same spot that he had started from, which made him laugh. Somebody had a sense of humour, he thought.

He was standing on the stone, that was once Captain Wirgoil's diary. He wanted to walk away but he couldn't, his feet were stuck to the stone!! He struggled, trying to free himself but the harder he struggled the softer the ground became. It quickly became quicksand and he was sinking into the ground fast - there was nothing that he could do to save himself. He knew that he was surely going to die. Robert sank up to his head and started taking his last breaths.

He'd seen horrible things happen in this place - he'd seen supposedly live people turn into skeletons. He'd seen a sunken ship rise to the surface and take the tramp away. He'd seen a whole village disappear. And now here he was about to find out his own fate. He took one last breath and said his final 'goodbye' to the world. He sank through the ground - there was now no trace that he'd ever been here.

Robert, to his surprise, wasn't dead. He'd been sucked into the ground. It was pitch dark and eerily quiet, he didn't know where he was. He started feeling around the walls with his hands. Suddenly he touched something. He didn't know what it was but miraculously the room lit up. He could now see where he was and didn't much like it. He could see that he was in a crypt. At the end of the crypt was a substantial iron gate. It had a keyhole but no key. It was obvious to him that this gate would be the only way out of this awful place. But he wouldn't be able to get out without the key.

Robert looked on the treasure map for any kind of clue as to where the key might be. There was no sign of a key on the map. On the map was a drawing of the first stone laid - the instructions of what steps had to be taken. The only other thing on the map was a drawing of a sea shell that was located at the top right hand corner. Robert looked at the key hole on the iron gate. It did look like the shape of a sea shell. There were plenty of sea shells on the ground, so Robert started picking them up trying to find a match but none of them fitted. He couldn't see how it would be possible for a sea shell to be able to open up this gate, anyway.

Robert was getting desperate. He wanted to get out of this place. He started looking on the walls of the crypt to see if there were any clues to where this shell key was. There were twenty-two burial chambers. All had been sealed by a stone that had the inscription of the name and date of the death of the person in the chamber. He walked down the rows and read each inscription. On the thirteenth chamber was a name that caught his attention.

There was a person that was buried here, called Jack K Shelley. Robert could see immediately the word shell and the middle letter of this name was a K. It didn't take much imagination to work out that if you incorporated the letter "K" between Shell and "ey" -it would read Shell Key.

Robert reasoned that the shell key must be inside this man's tomb. He knew that he had nothing to lose, so he removed the sealing stone away from the chamber. Inside the chamber, as he had expected, were the remains of the person. In his skeletal hand was a sea shell made of metal.

Robert took the shell and held it up against the iron gate key hole - it appeared to be a perfect fit. He pushed the shell into the hole. Instantly the shell started to turn, he could hear a clicking noise as it was unlocking the gate. A few moments later the gate swung open. Robert walked through the gate.

 He was relieved to get out of this place but didn't know what was going to happen next. Everything always seemed to be a test - it was like a game but it was a deadly game.

Past the gate was a cave room. There was just enough light reflecting through for Robert to see.

He could see old caskets - a cloth cover was covering something. Robert pulled off the cover and repelled backwards in shock. The cover was hiding a skeleton which had been chained to all the caskets. It was the remains of a person wearing what looked like a Captain's hat. Robert read the name on the cap. It read that it was the captain of the CLEO-H.

Robert now thought that this must be the remains of Captain Nigel Wirgoil. The Captain had gold coins stuffed inside his mouth. Robert could also see gold coins still within the skeletal structure. It appeared that the Captain was made to eat them.

Robert wondered if this was the Captain's fate - he had been chained to the treasure that he cheated out of his men, and been made to eat some of it. The surviving crew had then put a curse on him which was the challenge. Nobody had ever been able to do it, so the captain had remained chained to his treasure for three hundred years. Robert knew that the challenge had now been fulfilled, so the Captain should be free, but he wasn't.

Robert hadn't yet opened up any of the caskets so he wasn't sure if there was treasure in them. He opened up one of the caskets. He was a bit apprehensive doing this because everybody who had seen the treasure was now dead. Inside the casket was treasure; every casket was full to the brim. Robert was aware that the Captain was looking at him. He could sense that he wanted to be parted from the treasure but he didn't know what would unlock the chain. The chain didn't have a break, it was continuous.

Robert noticed that the gold coins inside the Captain's mouth were exactly the same date as the coin that he had been given by the old lady - 1665. He put his hand into his pocket and took out the coin - it was the same date. Robert wondered if this coin had been once part of this treasure.

He, for no logical reason, placed the coin into the Captain's mouth. Instantly all the coins flew out of the Captain's body and went straight into one of the treasure chests. One coin came flying back at Robert. He caught it, and put it into his pocket.

The chain started to unlock from the caskets. The Captain was at last free. His skeletal body jerked up from the ground. He saluted Robert, and started to walk off. Robert stood there watching. He wasn't frightened. Everything that he had witnessed over the past few months had been incredible, so nothing now surprised him. The skeleton of Captain Wirgoil walked towards what appeared to be a solid stone wall. As he walked his bones were clonking together. There didn't appear to be any way out of this cave that Robert could see. The Captain lifted his skeletal hand and pointed to something on the wall. Robert went over to see what the Captain was pointing at. There was a "X" marked on the wall with writing around it. Robert read it. It read:

Open, open, open for me, I'm the one that set you free

Robert had no idea as to what this meant but he knew that by putting the coin in the Captain's mouth he had set him free. He had no choice but to touch the "X," because he was a prisoner as well. So he touched the "X" on the wall. Suddenly and somewhat surprisingly the "X" turned into a cross, and a small gap appeared in the wall. Captain Wirgoil walked through the gap, Robert quickly followed him. As soon as he was through the gap, it closed. It led into a narrow cave corridor which slowly ascended. Robert followed the Captain. Up and up it went until finally coming to another solid stone wall. Once again the Captain pointed his hand to something on the wall. It was an "X" again with writing around it. Robert read it. It read:

If you touch this X and are not the one you'll turn into a skeleton

Robert didn't like the sound of that - he knew that this had been probably set up by the last remaining crew of Captain Wirgoil. If there was a threat to his life it was likely to happen now. He knew that if he wasn't "the one," he could be killed, but so far everything had worked, so he took a deep breath and touched the "X." Instantly the "X" turned into a cross and a gap appeared in the wall. The Captain walked through. Robert followed very closely behind him. When they had walked through the gap, it closed. It was now a solid piece of rock.

They were now outside on the sandy beach. Robert was glad of that. The Captain walked without stopping, straight into the sea and was gone - all that was left of him was his hat that was floating on the waves like a boat. Robert hoped that he would finally be reunited with his wife, Christine, but he stood there wondering if this would be the end of Captain Wirgoil or the start of something else? As he was pondering over this, all thoughts of the treasure was out of his mind. All that he could think about now was home.

Chapter Ten: Robert Meets a Princess

Home for him had been London. Robert had been brought up by adopted parents, who were very kind people. He never knew his real parents, he'd been adopted as a baby. He never even knew if "Robert" was the name given by his adopted parents or his real parents. They never talked about it, and Robert never asked any questions. He lived with his adopted parents, until he was told that he had a terminal illness. Robert, like a wounded animal, left home and roamed the countryside in search of finding an idyllic place to die. He wanted to end his days somewhere with beauty, rather than the drab streets of London.

Robert didn't know it but the gold coin that the old woman had given to him had led him to Cornwall, and the village. Robert walked up the path and out of the cove. Once out, the pathway closed, and would never open again. He was really looking forward to being reunited with his adopted parents whom he hadn't seen for quite some time. They were very happy to see him and remarked how well he looked. Robert felt guilty that he had left them but he didn't want to burden them with his terminal illness.

Robert had a head full of unbelievable stories to tell them but they would just be stories, because he knew that nobody would believe him; it would all sound so ridiculous. Robert felt very well now and the meaning of what Christine had said in Captain Wirgoil's diary was in his mind.

He had wished to be well, instead of having the treasure. The diary stated that "his wish had been granted." Robert thought, could this really be true? He did feel well. He took his tests at the hospital, and had an anxious two weeks' wait to find out the results of the tests. The day finally arrived for his appointment to see the consultant.

The consultant had a smile on his face which Robert knew was a positive indication that there may be good news for him. The consultant told him that there was no sign of the cancer – he, of course, wasn't able to explain how the cancer had miraculously disappeared but Robert knew.

Over the next few months Robert became very interested in the story of Captain Wirgoil, the King of England's son, Prince George, and Princess Amber. He wanted to find out the origins of whom this treasure belonged to. He knew that the sad tale had started sometime around 1664. And that Captain Wirgoil had been sent by the king at the time to track down the pirates who had killed his son and future daughter-in-law but nobody at the time knew about the treasure. It appeared to have been kept a secret.

Robert studied the case. He eventually found out that the treasure was the dowry from the King of a very small country called Selino Land. The King's name was Borrie Bow. The dowry was for his Princess daughter to officially marry the King of England's second son. They had already married in a tribal ceremony but it wasn't recognised as a legitimate marriage under English law. They were coming to England on the merchant ship with the dowry when they were attacked by the pirates. The dowry was a huge gift- such was the importance King Borrie Bow put on the union of his daughter to the King of England son.

The King's son, Prince George, had been sent to Selino Land to try and secure the gold and diamond mining rights that these lands held for England. While there, he fell in love with the princess.

Robert read the sad tale. He now knew whom the treasure belonged to but still to the present day nobody knew its whereabouts, or if the treasure was a fact, or as some people believed, fiction. Robert knew the treasure was a fact and he knew where it was. Under English law as soon as he exposed the treasure it would become treasure trove but under treasure trove rules, if ownership was known the treasure could be returned back to its rightful owners.

Robert wasn't sure in historical terms who now owned the treasure. It was to be given to the King of England as dowry but the marriage was never carried out in England so in theory the treasure should belong to the people of Selino Land. Robert had enough knowledge of what had happened and he found out where Selino Land was located. He really wanted to go to Selino Land, so he made preparations to go there.

Although it was a small country Robert had no idea as to where he should head for, once there, but he noticed that there was a place named Amber town on the map of the country. It seemed logical to him that he should start from there. The journey would take several days by plane and boat. Robert set off a few weeks later, he was very excited to go to the land where the sad story had started from - he wondered what he would find there.

Several days later he finally arrived at Selino Land. The light aircraft that he was travelling in landed on a small runway in a jungle. Amber town, was a two-day trek on horse- back from where he had landed. When Robert arrived at Amber town he was met by people dressed in tribal clothing - on first impressions, it seemed to be very primitive here.

Amber town was more of a village than a town. It had wooden huts, and dirt paths as roads.

The people were looking at him very strangely. Robert thought that was because he was a European. The Selino Land people seemed to be a close knit community. Robert had the feeling that nothing much had changed here since the king's son had been here three hundred years ago.

The villagers were talking and pointing at Robert. He became anxious and felt a bit uncomfortable. He had no idea if they were friendly.

Suddenly six men came running towards him. Robert stood there rigid. He didn't know what was going to happen.

"What's wrong? Have I done something wrong? I've come here as a friend," Robert pleaded with them.

The six men didn't answer, Robert didn't know if they understood English.

"Do you understand English? I've come in peace," Robert yelled.

But they didn't answer. One of the men motioned his hand for Robert to follow them. He felt that he didn't have much of a choice. So he followed them. He was taken to a large wooden hut. The hut was covered on its exterior with tribal art made from wood but there was also beautiful jewellery. Robert recognised some of the jewellery - it was similar to what he had seen in the caskets.

All the villagers were covered with this tribal jewellery. Robert knew that this would be worth lots of money in his world but he hadn't come here to make his fortune. He had come here to return the ten caskets of treasure that he thought was rightfully theirs.

Although Robert felt threatened nobody had actually been aggressive toward him. He went inside the hut and was met by a middle-aged, grey haired man who was wearing a rather beautiful crown on his head. The crown appeared to be made of gold and was inlaid with stones, Robert thought that the stones might be diamonds. The man was wearing tribal clothing. He had several necklaces dangling from his neck that looked like they were made of gold.

Robert assumed that this must be the King. He instinctively bowed his head in respect, and offered his hand in friendship. The man shook Robert's hand and then did something very strange. He pinched Robert's nose. Robert didn't know what to do next. He didn't know if this was just a bit of fun or a tribal thing. The man stood there waiting for Robert to do something. Robert did the only thing that he thought he had to do. He squeezed the man's nose back. The man nodded his head in approval. It appeared that this was a tribal greeting in this Land.

Robert now knew that he had nothing to worry about, these people were friendly. The man motioned for Robert to sit down on the hut floor. Which he did. He hadn't spoken yet, so Robert had no idea what language these Selino Land people spoke. The man stared at Robert, and nodded his head like in approval of something but Robert didn't know what.

A few moments later the hut door opened and in walked a woman in her early twenties. She was dressed in a flowery, silk dress. She, too, was wearing beautiful necklaces and her long brown curly hair was brushed over the front of her slim body. Robert looked at her with his mouth wide open and was dribbling. Her beauty had stunned him.

"Hello sir, greetings from Selino Land. I'm Princess Jopola, and this is my father King Dalla Bow. Who might you be?" Robert didn't answer. He appeared to be dazed.

"Sir, sir, who are you?" Princess Jopola was staring into Robert's eyes. She was puzzled as to why he wasn't answering so she prodded him with her finger, which seemed to wake Robert up.

"Oh, I'm so sorry, were you talking to me? I was miles away - my, you're so beautiful! Look at your beautiful skin, and your hair, and your eyes."

Princess Jopola had light tanned skin, her hair was dark brown that shone, her eyes were green and her teeth were perfect, they sparkled like stars.

"Thank you for the compliments but who are you ? And what are you doing here? You're welcome, of course," said the princess staring at Robert, intensely.

"My name is Robert. Did you say you were a princess? What shall I call you? Er... Umm... would it be ma'am? Or, your Highness? Or..." Robert was rambling.

"Why don't you call me Jo?" said the princess, smiling.

"Oh alright, Jo." Robert was trying to think of what to say next but his brain was escorting his thoughts into a wilderness.

"Jo's a nice name, I knew a girl called Jo - her name was really Jean but I called her Jo."

"Why?" asked the princess looking puzzled.

"Because there was a song that I liked called Visions of Johanna sang by Bob Dylan. I thought that Johanna was a friendly name so I called her Jo, she didn't seem to mind."

Princess Jopola asked again, "Robert, what are you doing here?"

Robert hesitated. "It's a long, sad story, Jo, but I've come here for a reason. Are you aware of the tragic story of a princess who came from this country called Princess Amber? It was a long time ago - in fact, three hundred years ago. She married the King of England's son here but they were killed by pirates off the Cornish coast, England, in 1666. I've come from England to return something that rightfully belongs to the people of this country and which the princess was taking to England."

"Yes, we do know what happened Robert," said the princess in a soft voice. "What on earth would you have, that belongs to us from all that time ago?"

Robert didn't answer the princess question. He suddenly realised that the present king had the same name as the old king had hundreds of years ago, "Jo, are you related to Borrie Bow, and princess Amber by any chance? You have the same name."

"Yes I am, they were our ancestors."

"Oh," said Robert "I'm very sorry, I didn't think."

"It's not your fault Robert - it was a long time ago but it could never be forgotten of course, and it hasn't," said the princess curling a few strands of her hair with her fingers.

"Of course it can't," said Robert. "It's something very nasty, and it affected your country as well as mine."

"Now then Robert, what have you found that belongs to us?" The princess was keen to know.

Robert took a deep breath. "Um, I know for a fact, Jo, that the pirates who stole the dowry that your distant family was to give to the King of England never got to spend any of it - nobody ever did. The dowry was cursed. Whoever saw it never survived to spend it. The dowry still exists."

The princess was looking puzzled. "How do you know these things?"

"Because, I found the dowry, Jo. It has caused so many deaths, I feel that it has to be returned to its rightful owners. It belongs to you, Jo, your people."

Princess Jopola looked at her father. He motioned her to bend down so that he could whisper something to her.

"My father tells me to ask you, what would you like to do with the dowry?"

"I'm frightened of it, Jo," said Robert with a stern face. "I believe that greed was the cause of so many people to die for it. Maybe it's best to leave it where it is? But it's not my decision."

The princess listened to Robert's story but he could sense that something else was on her mind. All the time that he was talking to her she was looking at her father who had a huge smile on his face and he was constantly nodding his head like he was in approval of something.

"What's wrong?" asked Robert

"What do you mean?" asked the princess.

"Well, you're not listening to what I'm saying, you've got something else on your mind, and why does your father keep looking at me and smile and nod his head?"

"It's you Robert, you've come home."

"What? No, I've never been here before. How can I have come home, when I've never been here?" Robert was puzzled by the princess's statement.

"You've been here before Robert, believe me!" said the princess mysteriously.

"And it's not possible for you to return the dowry back to us."

"Yes it is, I know where it is," said Robert not knowing what the princess was talking about.

"No," said the princess "Nobody would ever be able to remove it from where it lies - you might know where it is Robert, but you wouldn't be allowed to take it."

"Come with me," Princess Jopola took hold of Robert's hand and went outside the hut. "Close your eyes," whispered the princess. "I've got something very important to show you that might explain things."

Robert closed his eyes and was led a short distance. Behind them was King Dalla Bow and most of the villagers who had gathered outside the hut. It was as if everybody knew that something special was about to happen.

"You can open your eyes now." Robert opened his eyes and stood there in shock at what he was looking at.

In front of him was a big bronze statue of a man and a woman. The woman was posed handing a coin to the man. Robert looked hard at the statue and then turned to face Jo and then he turned his eyes back to the statue. He then pointed at the female statue and then turned and pointed at Jo. "That's you!!" He then followed the same procedure but pointed at the male statue and then himself. "That's me!! This is impossible, it can't be me. I can understand it being you, because Princess Amber was your relation, but I'm not a relation to the king of England."

"How do you know you're not related to the King of England?" said Princess Jopola.

"Do you know who your mother and father were?"

"Well, no. I don't, I was adopted as a baby. I've never known who my parents were, so I suppose it could be possible that hundreds of years ago I had some royal blood in my family. What made you think that? It's a strange thing to say."

Princess Japola just shrugged her shoulders, and didn't answer the question.

The princess then pointed her finger at the plinth of the statue for Robert to read. There was an inscription which read:

In memory of Princess Amber

And Prince George

Killed by pirates off the coast of Cornwall, England

May their souls rest in peace

Presented by the King of England to the people of Selino Land

1675

The statue was that of Princess Amber and Prince George. The princess was handing the prince a coin. There was another small inscription on the statue which read:

Return this coin to me and everything will be as it should be

Robert immediately realised that the second inscription was what the old lady had said to him when she gave him the gold coin. He turned to the princess, "What is the coin, Jo?"

The princess explained to Robert that the coin was a specially designed gold coin that was presented to Prince George by King Borrie Bow to mark the year that his daughter was to be officially married in England. The coin was dated 1666 and had the head of Prince George on one side and the head of Princess Amber on the other. She told him that it was believed the pirates stole it from the prince - it has never been seen since. Only the return of the coin can return the dowry.

"But how did the King of England know about the coin?" asked Robert.

"King Borrie Bow told the king of England about the dowry and the special gold coin. Years afterwards he wanted to get it back and believed that if the coin was found - so too would be the dowry. We've always believed that this would happen."

Robert thought about this. He still had the gold coin that the old woman had given to him in his pocket, but he knew that it didn't have the faces of Princess Amber and Prince George stamped on it. A lot of coins had flown out of Captain Wirgoil's skeletal body. One coin was returned back to him. He didn't know if he'd got back the same coin as the old woman had given to him but he knew that it wasn't the coin that the princess was referring to, because he'd looked at it loads of times. He had even showed his adopted parents the coin. It was definitely a 1665 coin.

Robert always carried the coin, as a good luck charm. He took the coin out of his pocket and looked at it, and went pale.

"What's wrong Robert?" asked the princess. "Are you unwell?"

"I'm alright Jo. I've just had a bit of a shock. You won't believe this but I've got the gold coin that you've been talking about. Look!" Robert showed the princess the coin. She agreed that it was the special coin.

"I don't understand this," said Robert shaking his head. "How can a coin change into a different coin? This is madness, what on earth is going on?"

"Where did you get that coin from?" The princess looked shocked herself.

"I got it from an old..." Robert paused, because he wasn't sure now. "... I was going to say that I got it from an old woman but this may not be the coin that she gave to me - this coin came from the skeletal body of Captain Wirgoil. He had possession of the dowry."

"Who is Captain Wirgoil?" asked the princess.

Robert realised that nobody knew what had happened to Captain Wirgoil.

"He was the Captain of a ship sent out to escort the merchant ship that was attacked by the pirates that killed Princess Amber and Prince George. He survived the attack and was the only person who knew where the pirates had attacked the ships from, which turned out to be a secret cove with a village.

He was sent by the King of England to find and kill the pirates but when he got there, the pirates had all killed each other for the treasure. The Captain, four members of his crew, and his wife Christine also succumbed to the treasure's lure. He told his men that he would give them a share of the treasure but he put sea-shells in ten sacks pretending them to be part of the treasure, and then attacked them.

Captain Wirgoil was killed, along with everybody who had ever seen this treasure.

The curse was the challenge. It was put on the treasure by the last remaining crew of Captain Wirgoil. Whoever accepted the challenge had to collect sea-shells for food, Jo, and if you collected enough shells you were told that you would win the treasure, but the challenge was impossible unless it was done by two people, and one had to sacrifice himself for the other, which nobody was ever prepared to do. The challenge was based on greed.

I fulfilled the challenge Jo, because I sacrificed myself. I realised that at one point there were always two people in the village. I knew from the start that the challenge was impossible for one person to do, but if the last person to accept the challenge was willing to sacrifice himself ,it could be fulfilled by the other person. That's what I did. By sharing my shells with the other man, it was possible for the challenge to be fulfilled.

I was the one who solved the challenge, Jo, without realising it, so I was led to the treasure by a treasure map. I found the treasure and released Captain Wirgoil from the curse by placing a gold coin into his mouth. Loads of coins flew out of his body but I hadn't realised that the coin that I placed into his mouth wasn't the coin that was returned to me. Captain Wirgoil's treasure was just sea shells - nobody was ever going to get the real treasure. What do I do with the coin, Jo?"

Princess Jopola had an idea of what had to be done.

"Um, now, let me think. It says that the coin has to be returned -

Return this coin to me and everything will be as it should be

You have to give the coin back, it belongs to Prince George. I think that you have to place the gold coin on top of the statue coin."

Robert went up to the statue and placed the coin over the coin on the statue - it was twenty times smaller than the statue's coin. The gold coin seemed to stick to it like a magnet. A few moments later, the gold coin started to rotate on the bronze coin. It moved faster and faster until it was just a blur.

The village people cheered. Robert and the princess stood and watched in amazement at what was happening. Suddenly the hand of Princess Amber appeared to move. Her bronze hand, handed the gold coin to the prince. Once again the villagers cheered. They knew that something truly remarkable was taking place. The bronze statue started to smoke, and then slowly started to fragment into thousands of pieces. Suddenly a dark cloud came over and blocked out the sun. It was very murky.

The villagers, King Dalla Bow, Princess Jopola and Robert - all stepped back away from the statue. There was a loud bang followed by a big puff of smoke. All the pieces of the statue shot up into the air. Thousands of pieces of the statue suddenly exploded in a mass of colours (like fireworks going off) which lit up the sky. The coloured fragments seemed to form into groups as they came drifting back to earth. It was now so smoky that nobody could see what was happening but the sounds of something hitting the ground where the statue used to be could clearly be heard.

The dark cloud moved away from the sun - it was a nice sunny day again now. The smoke slowly cleared. The statue was gone but in its place were ten caskets. Robert recognised the caskets as the ones that he had found in Cornwall. He couldn't imagine how it was possible for the caskets to be here, thousands of miles from where he had last seen them but he'd seen many things that couldn't possibly be explained.

He'd seen skeletal people walk and talk, and a sunken ship rise from the sea- bed, taking the tramp away. He'd seen a village disappear, and his coin had changed into a different coin. He knew that none of these happenings would ever be able to be explained, but they had happened - that was a fact. And today, a solid bronze statue had fragmented into the precious items that was once the dowry. He didn't understand how Princess Jopola knew that he wouldn't be able to remove the dowry from the cave but she was right. The dowry found its way home by itself. The King of England had been correct - the return of the special coin did return the dowry. Robert couldn't imagine how this was all possible.

He opened one of the caskets to make sure that it did contain the treasure. As expected, it did. They all did. The people of Selino Land had finally got their valuable items back. There was loud cheering followed by clapping from the village people. They knew that something remarkable had taken place that day.

Out of the crowd came forward an old lady, "Here," she said, "these belong to you. Everything will soon be back as it once was." She took her ring off her finger and handed it to Robert, along with a gold coin. The old lady appeared to be getting younger. Robert felt sure that he had heard this voice before. He was certain that it was the same woman who had given him the gold coin in London.

"Haven't we met before?" Robert asked the woman. "Didn't you give me the coin?"

"Maybe I did - maybe I didn't," replied the woman mysteriously. She seemed to be getting younger and younger in front of Robert's eyes.

"It doesn't matter now. Everything is nearly alright, my soul will soon rest in peace - it's been a long hard battle, George."

"No, ma'am, I'm not George, my name is Robert."

"No, you're George, you've mistaken yourself. Thank you for putting things right. I knew that you would. Give this ring to the princess. It belongs to her now, she's my soul. You gave it to me a long time ago, and I gave you the coin, do you remember?"

"No ma'am, it wasn't me," said Robert, baffled by the woman's statement. She seemed to be rambling. Robert had no idea what she was talking about.

The old woman was now not old at all. She was young and beautiful, she looked the image of Princess Jopola. She leant over and gave Robert a kiss.

"It's time for me to go but I won't be long. We'll be together soon, my darling." Then she disappeared. Robert wasn't sure whether she had ever really been there but he had in his hand the ring and the coin.

Princess Jopola came up to Robert. "Why are you talking to yourself?" she asked, pondering.

"Um..." Robert was thinking about what had just taken place. He paused his thoughts for a moment.

"... I wasn't talking to myself, Jo." he spoke slowly, and softly.

"Yes, you were. I was watching you, and you were mumbling something. What's all that about?"

Robert stood there, not really knowing what was going on.

"I know that you won't believe me but I was talking to an old lady who turned into you."

The princess laughed. "Don't be so ridiculous, how could you have been talking to an old woman who turned into me?

That's really silly," said the princess looking into Robert's eyes. "Where did you get that lipstick from, that's on your face?" The princess pointed her finger to the spot.

"She kissed me, and said it was time for her to go but she said that she would comeback soon. She disappeared in front of my eyes. She was here, Jo. She gave me something to give to you. She said that I had given it to her but I hadn't, she's mistaken me for somebody else. I think that she was the woman who gave me the coin in London. It's all a bit of a mystery. Things are happening that can't be explained. I feel that I've been in the middle of something that's incredible but it's nearing the end now. Here, this is for you."

Robert opened up his clenched hand to reveal the ring. The princess looked at it and shook her head.

"This can't be."

"What can't be, Jo?"

"It can't be. It's impossible!" The princess was shaking her head.

"You've said that already, what can't be?"

"The ring, Robert. Where did you get it?"

"I told you. I got it from the old lady who turned into you. She told me that everything is alright now - it was definitely the same woman who gave me the coin because I recognised that ring. She was wearing it. It's unusual. It's amber, and it has a fly embedded within it. Look at it, Jo. Isn't it unusual? And she gave me this coin. It's the same gold coin that I put into the statue."

"Oh God!" muttered the princess.

"What's wrong, Jo?"

"You couldn't have got the ring from the old lady."

"Why?"

"Because this ring belonged to Princess Amber. She was buried here in Selino Land in this very village that now bears her name. She was wearing the ring when she was buried. Prince George gave it to her. So how can you have it? It's not possible."

"Oh," said Robert. "I don't know but she did give it to me. I've got a feeling that Princess Amber is trying to put everything right."

The Princess took hold of Robert's hand and led him to the cemetery. He was taken to Princess Amber's grave.

Despite the gravestone being three hundred years old, it had the appearance that it had just been placed there - Robert had the feeling that everything was going backwards.

There was a message on the headstone that only he could read. It read:

The ring must touch your hearts

There was also a message that only Princess Jopola could read. It read:

The coin must be given

Robert took the ring off the princess and placed it on her finger. Instantly the amber on the ring started to glow and pulsate like a beating heart. He then asked the princess to touch his heart with the ring. Which she did without asking why. He then told her to touch her own heart with the ring. Which she did. Once again she didn't ask why. Robert embraced the princess and kissed her. They both shuddered. It was like somebody else's souls had entered their bodies. They held the embrace for several minutes.

The villagers and King Dalla Bow clapped and cheered. They had followed them to the cemetery. The princess knew what she had to do. She handed the gold coin to Robert. As soon as it was in his hand something dramatic happened. All the writing on Princess Amber's gravestone started to run down it. The solid marble stone started to melt like it was made of ice. In just a few moments the grave of Princess Amber was gone. It felt like it had never existed.

Robert kissed the princess. "We're back together now," he said lovingly.

He looked extremely happy at this moment in time and was smiling at the princess.

Robert knew that everything was back to the beginning. It was the end of the adventure to be re-united with his princess.

*

He closed his eyes and took a deep breath. Suddenly he felt very faint - his mind started to drift into a deep sleep. Bright coloured lights started flashing in his brain. Then everything went blank.

George looked to be at peace lying in his hospice bed. His son, Nigel, and Nigel's wife, Christine, were at his bedside to witness George take his last breath of life. The cancer that he had been fighting for over a year, finally took its toll on his weakened body. Sadly George, had *-lost the challenge.*

George's limp right hand slipped off the bed sheet, and dangled from the bed. Two items dropped out of his hand, and fell onto the floor. Nigel bent down and picked them up. He was surprised to see that his dad had been clutching onto an amber ring and a gold coin.

"He must have thought a lot of these items," said Christine.

"Yes he did.." said Nigel. "They were my mother and father's wedding gifts to each other.

Dad bought the amber ring and mum bought dad the special gold coin."

A male nurse who had been looking after Nigel's dad came to his bedside and switched off **Wirgoil,** the life support system, that had been keeping him alive for the last few days of his life.

The male nurse's name was Peter Bradshaw.

The ward doctor who had looked after him during his short stay at the hospice came into the ward. He had one last task to perform. He had to write out the medical certificate as to the cause of death.

With his pen in his hand he wrote the words on the document.

Ambertown Hospice: Selino Ward
He wrote:

George Robert Bow:
Died at 1:13pm on14th November 1970. Age 78
Cause of death: Brain cancer.
Signed by: Doctor K. Shelley

Doctor Shelley told Nigel and Christine that George's mind was very confused in the last few days of his life. He told them that George was rambling and waving his arms around, and he was mumbling strange things about princesses, treasure, and gold coins, and he kept on shouting out the challenge is impossible, don't bother to collect the shells.

Nigel was baffled as to why his dad would be saying these strange things but reasoned that it must have been the condition of his brain. As Dr Shelley was explaining Nigel's father's state of mind, they could hear a squeaking noise coming down the corridor.

"What's that squeaking noise?" asked Nigel.

"Oh, it's only Albert," said the doctor. "He's doing his tea round, that old tea trolley that he uses has got a squeaky wheel. I don't know how many times I've asked him to put a bit of oil on that wheel, but he doesn't listen to me. He must like the sound of it."

The doctor poked his head out of the corridor.

"Albert, can you oil that wheel, please, you're disturbing the patients."

"I don't know what you're complaining about, doctor?" said Albert. "George loved the sound of that squeaky wheel. He told me so before he became very ill. He said that he always knew when the tea was coming."

Nigel and Christine left the hospice with tears in their eyes but at the same time they were happy that George would now be re-united with his late wife, Nigel's mother, Amber Jopola Bow. Whom, they knew, he missed very much.

Outside the hospice, Nigel handed the amber ring to Christine.

"This belongs to you now. I know that my mother would want you to have it."

Christine put the ring on her finger. It seemed to glow suddenly brighter in the weak November sunshine.

An old lady who was standing outside the hospice had a charity box in her hand. She was collecting money for food for the poor.

"Can you spare a few coppers, sir?" she asked politely.

Nigel put his hand in his pocket and pulled out the gold coin and put the coin in the box.

"Thank you so much," said the old lady. "That is very generous and kind of you."

Nigel smiled and said, "I know that this is what my father would have wanted. He was a kind man and cared about people."

Christine smiled at Nigel. She just knew that this was the right thing to do.